Tess

Annie Seaton

Pentecost Island Series: 9

Dedication

To those women who are brave enough to stand up for what they believe in… and break the glass ceiling in their careers.

Acknowledgements

A special thank you to my wonderful editor and critique partner, Susanne Bellamy, and my eagle-eyed proof-reader, Roby Aiken.

Prologue

Tess

Tess closed the desk drawer beneath the reception counter and locked it. She looked at the key in her hand, thinking locking the drawer was probably overkill in the office at Ma Carmichael's resort on Pentecost Island, but events in her former working life had led to a huge lack of trust. Taking the key through to the back office behind reception, she hung it on the hook behind the filing cabinet.

Tess was in a place where she knew she was safe. Looking around the office, she smiled. She loved working here and knew she had found the right solution for her life. Her healing had begun, her confidence had returned; Tess knew she was respected by the rest of the staff—male and female. She was treated kindly and, best of all, she had forged new friendships with women who liked her for who she was, and not what she had or what she could do for them. She would be forever grateful to Cherry for recommending her for the office position on Pentecost Island after they had met up again on Hamilton Island. They had clicked as they had worked together in the bar and when they moved into a shared apartment, Cherry was an easy roommate.

Working as a casual housemaid on Pentecost Island before she started work in the office had been okay—it was a job, and on an isolated island—but when the part-time office work job had turned into a traineeship, Tess had been ecstatic. Working on the island was the first step in a new career. With Nell being pregnant, there was a chance she would be promoted while her boss was on maternity leave.

Tess had finished up the day's work in the office, and offered to stay for lock up so Nell could get ready for the staff Christmas party. Nell finished the check ins, and headed off while Tess ran the reports in the back office.

The file server whirred in the background; being Saturday, it was a weekly backup as well, and the run would take a bit longer. Tess glanced at her watch; she had time for a quick call home while she waited for the reports to back up to the cloud and the file server that Nell's partner Nat had installed a couple of weeks ago. She pulled out her mobile and pressed the speed dial for home. They would have had dinner by now and Mum would be in the kitchen cleaning up while Dad watched the news and the boys went to the pub.

Home was as predictable as sunrise and sunset, as was the time it took for Mum to pick up the call.

'Hi, Mum.'

'Hello, love. I was going to call you later. We haven't talked for a couple of weeks.'

'Sorry, it's been really hectic here. And I've started my online course, and that keeps me busy at night.'

'Are you good? Are you eating properly?'

Tess smiled. 'Yes, I am. I love living on the island and the new job's fantastic. And I've put a bit of weight on too. The food here is too good.'

'I'm just pleased that you're not working in those rough hotels anymore. I didn't sleep the whole year you lived at the Gold Coast. Isn't it about time you came home?'

Tess rolled her eyes. Just like the predictability of a day in her family home, her mother's conversation would go down the same track it always did. She waited for the "are you getting eight hours sleep every night" question, but was surprised when Mum hesitated and cleared her throat.

'Theresa? I wasn't going to tell you this, but your father told me I had to.'

'What, Mum? Are you all right? You're not sick, are you?'

Her mother's laugh boomed over the phone. 'Gawd, no, love. I'm as fit as a mallee bull.' She hesitated again, and Tess waited.

'So what do you have to tell me?'

'That . . . that man has been looking for you. He rang here twice asking to speak to you and then he turned up. Dad had to get the boys to the door to convince him he wasn't welcome.'

'You didn't tell him where I am, did you?' Tess's skin started to crawl and she fought the urge to scratch. She'd done enough of that in the middle of the worst time two years ago.

'No. I'm not silly, love. I recognised his voice. It's a lovely voice, deep and quite sexy, isn't it?'

'Mum!'

'Sorry . . . but he did take me in the first time I met him, but now I know how he treated you, I'll give him what for if he shows his snooty rich nose back here. If you'd been charged, I reckon your Dad and the boys would have gone after him. It was all his doing.'

'So no one said I'm in Queensland, did they?'

Her mother cackled. 'No, but the boys were ready for him. Ted let slip that you were in Exmouth in Western Australia. They put on a good show. When he did that, Dad clipped his ear and told him he was a dickhead. Hopefully the tosser's gone off on a wild goose chase now.'

'How long ago was this?' Tess's scalp *was* crawling now.

'Oh, about six weeks ago. I wasn't going to tell you, but Dad's been onto me every time I hang up the phone from you. Just so you watch your back, he said.'

'Thanks. Mum and say thanks to Dad for me. Tell him this place is almost like Fort Knox, and being in reservations, I get to see the guests' names before they arrive. If *he* turned up, I'd scarper.'

'Good. You might come home.'

Tess sighed. 'No, Mum, but I'd have to hide again. I'm over it. I feel safe here. You should come here for a holiday.'

Her mother's laugh boomed over the phone, and Tess felt slightly better. Her family had her back, that was for sure.

'Ha, can you see your father on a beach, and me in a bikini?'

This time Tess couldn't stop the smile tugging at her lips. 'I can, Mum.'

'One more thing. Have you told anyone there what happened? So they know to watch your back too?'

'God, no. I'm making a totally fresh start. I'm happy, and I'm well. And I'm safe here. That's all you need to worry about.'

'Maybe you should tell one person. That Cherry girl was a good friend to you on the Gold Coast.'

'No, Mum. There's no need. Listen, I have to go now. We have the staff Christmas party tonight. Say hello to Dad and the boys for me.'

'I will, and you look after yourself, love. The chooks miss you too. They haven't laid anywhere near as well since you left.'

Tess could always depend on Mum to bring a smile to her face, although this smile was brief. The call had shaken her, but forewarned was forearmed. She'd covered her tracks really well when she'd left her job in Sydney; even the media hadn't found her on the Gold Coast. She'd been big news in Sydney for a couple of weeks, and when she'd disappeared, they'd left her in peace as someone else had made the news. Tess lifted one hand to her head and ruffled her short-cropped hair.

I will not scratch!

Trying to forget Mum's words, she convinced herself she was all right.

I am.

She was safe here, but no, she wasn't going to tell anyone her past history. She hadn't been charged, and she'd left the city, and it was no-one's business.

As Tess closed the office door—and locked it—the music from the restaurant drifted across through the glade. It lifted her spirits; there was no point being down. What was in the past would stay there. What upset her the most was despite what he'd done, she still missed him and dreamed about him some nights.

The disco beat pulsed through the forest; Pippa was obviously in charge of the music selection The girls had been teasing Pippa—her boss and owner of the resort—about her music tastes the other day when they'd gathered for sunset drinks on the beach to welcome Sienna, the day spa therapist, back from her time away at a course on another island further north.

Tess's foot began to tap and

before she reached the end of the veranda she was dancing, singing along with the music as the song changed to *I Will Survive.* That had become her theme song over the past two years.

Before she reached the turn leading to the side veranda, she stopped dancing, stood straight and put on her professional face. She looked down at her uniform and debated whether to get changed. Yes, she would; tonight she'd let her hair down, have a few drinks and enjoy herself. Every night her eyes scanned the booking sheets for the following day, reassuring herself that she would not be found.

At least it was better here than when she'd been doing bar and hospitality work on the Gold Coast. Every night there, her eyes roamed over the bar patrons, terrified she would see a familiar face.

But the people she'd worked with in Sydney wouldn't be frequenting cheap bars on the Gold Coast; they had more upmarket tastes. Her hair was now short and blonde; her long dark hair had been chopped off the day after she arrived at Coolangatta. She'd worried about the three new piercings in her ears, but Pippa hadn't cared.

'Looks fine to me,' her boss had said with a grin when Tess checked. 'As long as you do your work well, and fit in with the rest of us, I don't care what colour hair you have, or how many earrings you wear. We're pretty laidback here.'

Tess grinned as she walked along the veranda. Blonde hair,

pierced ears and blue contact lenses. Her parents wouldn't even recognise her She could just imagine what they would say if they ever saw her new look. Dad would be unbearable.

She shook her head. It was a new look, but it would be a *temporary* one. Another couple of years, when she was convinced all was well, she'd grow her hair back. She missed long hair brushing on her shoulders.

Before Tess headed to her room, she checked that the guests at the temporary restaurant on the veranda were being looked after by the casual restaurant staff over from Hamo. Jiminy was coming at midnight to take them back across the Passage with the rest of the staff who'd come over for the staff function.

'Sounds like a good Christmas party,' an older gentleman sitting with his wife said as Tess paused to speak to them. 'We used to disco dance when we were young, didn't we, love?'

His wife laughed. 'I danced, Reg. I recall you propping up the bar. You hated dancing!'

Tess smiled at them and went into the kitchen. 'All good in here, guys?' she asked.

'Yep,' Greg, the temporary chef replied. 'Mains are done and cleared, dessert's about to go out.'

'Great, thanks. Pippa said to make sure you all come over for a drink before Jiminy arrives later. And thanks for stepping in. It meant that all the staff here could have a night off.'

'What about you? You're working,' he said moving a bit too

close for her comfort.

'Me? I'm going to the party now.'

'Save me a seat, I'll have a drink with you.'

Tess flashed him a non-committal smile, and hurried out of the kitchen and down the back steps.

Her time for romance was done. Casual or long term. Her experience in Sydney had put paid to any dreams of marriage, kids, the white picket fence, and the lemon tree in the backyard. To have that, you had to have trust, and Tess had not one skerrick of that left in her.

Burned once, never again.

This traineeship on Pentecost Island was a new start for her; the beginning of a new career and she was going to give it one hundred percent.

Hurrying to her room, and keeping an eye out for anyone loitering, Tess had a quick wash, changed her clothes, and put on some lipstick. She hadn't eaten since lunchtime and the aroma of the curries the casual staff had put on for the guests had made her stomach grumble. Pulling her door shut behind her, she made her way along the back lawn to the glade.

The first staff Christmas party on Pentecost Island was in full swing.

The music was louder and had that great beat, and through the trees she could see half a dozen couples on the dance floor. As she walked along the path, she was sure it was Rafe who dipped Pippa almost to the floor in a fancy move. Sienna and Danny were cheek to cheek dancing slowly, despite the disco beat. The tables were full of happy people speaking loudly over the music. Pippa had brought the housemaids and kitchenhands over from Hamo for the party.

It was going to be a great night and Tess was looking forward to letting her hair down for the first time in a couple of years. Well, maybe not her hair, but she'd let her guard down and relax.

And by God, she needed that. The past two years of bar work—where she had met Cherry on the Gold Coast and then followed her to Hamilton Island—had been hard work and so different to what she was used to, but Tess had needed that sort of job to recover. It might not have been exactly what she was qualified for—an honours degree in economics wasn't exactly a prerequisite for bar work. When she'd been knocked back for the first jobs she'd applied for, Tess had soon learned not to mention her qualifications or where she'd previously worked. After the early sceptical receptions she'd received, she'd soon learned to mention only the waitressing and bar work she'd done when she was at uni.

But as hard as it was, the work on the Gold Coast and Hamilton Island had been for a reason, and had eventually brought her to Pentecost Island.

She hurried through the glade and was almost to the bar when someone stepped from the rainforest and blocked her way.

'Theresa.'

Tess put her hand to her throat as her past came rushing

back to her with that one simple word. Her name whispered in that deep voice. The voice that had once sent pleasant shivers down her back. Now it was sheer terror that caused the shiver that made her whole body shake. Her ears buzzed, and Tess stepped back as fear consumed her.

She struggled to speak. 'What the hell are you doing here?'

'I'll tell you but first I need you to keep a secret. Please don't tell anyone who I am.'

Her nemesis stepped closer to her and Tess shrunk away, fighting the faintness that threatened to consume her.

Chapter 1
Two years earlier - Sydney

Theresa Anderson took a deep breath, pushed her umbrella up and stepped out onto George Street. An autumn southerly buster had come barrelling in from the Antarctic just before five o'clock and the gutters in the city were already running like creeks that reminded her more of home than the city.

She stepped onto the wet pavement and shivered as a strong gust of icy wind turned her umbrella inside out and rendered it useless.

That'd be right. A rotten end to a rotten day. Pulling a face as she muttered a curse, Theresa shoved the cheap umbrella into the nearest bin, put her head down and headed for Wynyard Station. She wasn't looking forward to the long train trip out to Brentwood tonight; her clothes were drenched already, and the air conditioning in the train was always too cold. The last thing she needed was a head cold.

With a sigh, she strode out. As much as it would be more convenient to live closer to the city, Theresa simply couldn't afford it.

Not being able to stay in the office and work back really peed her off. Even though she was the first assistant to the executive officer on the trading floor, she hadn't reached a senior enough level to be allowed to stay in the office after five. It was a ridiculous policy. If she was allowed to, she could have waited until the rain had eased, finished the international transaction she was working on and taken the late train home. As she'd worked through the afternoon, Theresa had lost track of the time, and when the five o'clock bell had rung, she'd been in the middle of a complex foreign transfer.

'Shit,' she'd muttered. If she logged off now, she'd have to start again on Monday.

'What's up, Reeza?' Boyd Drummond, the trader opposite her—and son of the CEO of the bank—looked at her around his computer screen.

'I didn't realise the time and I have to leave this Swiss Bank transaction.'

'Don't worry, stay logged in and I'll finish it off for you. Is that the Zurich one?'

'It is.'

'Okay, you get going, and I'll sort it.' Boyd stood, and not for the first time, Theresa repressed the revulsion that his cold eyes always sent running through her. She was also aware of the admiration in his eyes, and the way he would stand closer than necessary to her in the small alcove where they always seemed to arrive at the same time.

It made her very uncomfortable.

Theresa was focused on making her way up to a senior position, and there was no way she would compromise that by going out with anyone in the bank. Or responding to Brad's frequent flirting, even if he was the CEO's son. Any promotion she got, she would earn by exemplary work.

'Thanks, appreciate your offer,

Brad, but it's okay. It can wait until Monday.' Reeza forced herself to smile at him, but not so much that he took it as a come on. She reached down and grabbed her bag, slipped on the high heels that she'd kicked off beneath her desk after the last coffee break, and headed for the lift that would take her from the top of the skyscraper near the harbour, and down to George Street.

Being a Friday evening the crowd from the bars would usually spill out onto the street, but because of the rain, the patrons were crammed at tables beneath the awnings. And that meant that most of her walk to the station was in the drenching, cold rain. Within minutes her black corporate suit was sodden, her shoes were ruined and her hair was plastered to the sides of her cheeks. Theresa's foul temper worsened, as she tottered along on her four inch heels and stepped into a deep puddle where the gutter had overflowed into a dip on the footpath.

'Bloody hell.' She stopped, pulled her shoes off, tucked them beneath her arm and walked along in wet stockinged feet. Those shoes had been her one splurge this year—she hadn't been able to resist them—and she might as well put them in the bin with the umbrella now.

As she reached Jamison Street, she turned up the steep hill, grateful for the overhanging roof of the hotel that kept the rain off. The regular concierge smiled as she passed and she looked down, a glimmer of a smile breaking through her bad mood.

'Evening, Theresa.'

'Evening, John. Have a good weekend.'

'You too.' His grin was wider than usual.

I must look a right sight, she thought.

Five minutes later, Theresa was through the station, her Opal card safely back in her purse and settled into a seat in the middle carriage.

She pulled her phone out.

Pick me up at Brentwood Station at 7.15 pls, she texted home.

Sorry no can do. Picking, came straight back from Ted. **You'll have to leg it, sis.**

Mum? she sent back.

Out, was the reply.

Raining? she asked.

'No, just the bloody wind.

Peaches are falling at the rate of knots. Dad has the shits.

Just what she needed. A walk home and a cranky father on arrival. With a bit of luck he'd go to the pub after they finished picking. Tess put her head back on the damp cushion of the high backed seat and closed her eyes, letting the movement of the train soothe her as it pulled out of the station right on time.

She'd worry about how to get to the farm when she got off the train. Maybe it was time to consider moving closer to the city. Maybe a share house in the inner western suburbs would be affordable.

Maybe.

##

Two hours later, Theresa's suit had dried a little from the air conditioning on the train but it had been an unpleasant trip; she'd shivered most of the way. She'd changed trains at Campbelltown to get the Intercity train to Brentwood and now, after another half an hour, the train finally approached her station. She slipped her still wet shoes back on and made her way to the automatic door. The train was almost full, as commuters made their way to Melbourne for the weekend.

She peered through the glass door as the train approached the station. At least the rain had only been coastal, the trees were swaying in the strong southerly wind as they entered the small township. That's why Dad and the boys would be out picking. With a wind like this, the last of the peach crop would be at risk.

Theresa stepped off the train and crossed her fingers there would be a taxi at the rank. But of course in line with the rest of the day, the street was empty, and there was no sign of a taxi.

Maybe Mum was in town at a meeting, she thought. She could find her car, and use the spare key that was in a magnetised container under the back mudguard, and then come back later and pick Mum up. Pulling out her phone, she pressed the speed dial for Mum, thinking how ridiculous it was that a woman of twenty-nine years of age was ringing her mother to try and get home.

Home to the family farm where she'd grown up and had never left. When her friends had moved into the city to go to uni, Theresa had opted to stay at home and work on the family stone fruit orchard. Money had always been tight in the seasonal industry that was so dependent on the weather each summer.

Three years later, she decided that she was going to go to uni and do the study she had always wanted to pursue. The train commute to uni three days a week was the price she'd paid for wanting to save, as she studied for her economics degree.

Dad had stared at her as though she had two heads when she'd announced she was going to uni on the night of her twenty-first birthday. 'Why the hell would you do that? There's plenty of work for you in the orchard.'

'No. I want to have a career,' she'd said.

He'd shaken his head. 'We

can't afford it.'

'It won't cost you anything, Dad. I'll live at home, and I'll work in the shed on the days I don't have lectures.'

'Whatever.' His attitude hadn't improved over the six years it had taken her to complete her degree, and her honours years. She had worked in the shed and in the orchard and held down two part-time jobs in town Even landing a job at one of the biggest trading banks in the country when she'd graduated hadn't impressed her father. Nor did the fact that she had a huge HECS debt to pay back for her university course.

No wonder her desire to get away to the city and live there was so strong. There was a whole world out there for Theresa to see, and she now had a job that had kickstarted her career in finance and gave her the salary she needed to be a part of that world.

A world where she wasn't standing in a packing shed grading peaches and apricots, or out in the hot summer sun pruning trees.

But Theresa was not a risktaker, and she was frugal and sensible with her spending and saving. As soon as she'd paid off her HECS debt, she would move to the city. She figured it would take another three months, and then she could maybe consider it. Excitement rippled through her.

And then her life would begin in the city.

The *inner* city where one day she'd have a swanky apartment with white carpet, her *own* huge television for watching what she wanted when she wanted and not have to fight with her brothers for the remote or use her phone to watch Netflix. She would have an all-white bathroom with a heart-shaped spa bath, and a state of the art kitchen with a coffee machine.

Dream on, girl, she told herself as she waited for her mother to pick up the call, but there was no answer.

With a sigh, she called Ted, her oldest brother. He answered straight away.

'Can you pick me up in town when you finish picking please?' she asked. 'There's no taxis around.

'We'll be a couple of hours yet.'

'Where's Mum?'

'At a meeting in Thirlmere.'

'Okay. I'll grab some dinner at the Federal and wait for you there.'

'Hang on.'

She could hear Ted talking to someone and rolled her eyes when he came back and told her what was happening.

'Dad said he'll pick you up in an hour.'

Great, just what she needed. Another lecture on how selfish she was.

'Thank you. I'll be in the bistro.'

Theresa disconnected the call, and as she set off for the hotel two kilometres away, the sky opened and it began to bucket down.

Maybe Dad was right. Maybe she was a fool.

Chapter 2

Zac Montgomery turned off the Hume Highway onto the narrow country road. Anticipation built as his black BMW purred along, leading him towards the small town of Brentwood. This weekend he was going to find his new home in the country. The windscreen wipers swished back and forward rhythmically and Zac yawned. An accident on the M5 had held him up for an hour, and another big day at the bank had taken its toll. Dinner, a whisky and bed were looking very attractive. The weather forecast for the weekend ahead wasn't boding well for an outdoor auction, and a tinge of disappointment dampened his anticipation slightly. He'd been looking forward to trudging over the grassy hills, checking the property out before the auction. They'd have to move the auction to the office. He was determined to look the place over first. The auction wasn't until early afternoon and hopefully the rain would ease overnight. It would be a pain if this heavy rain didn't let up.

The railway station flashed by on his right and Zac peered ahead looking for the turnoff to the main part of town where the hotels were located. Flicking on his GPS he keyed in the hotel and the route came up. He'd grab a pub meal before he checked into the motel which he knew was simply a room with basic facilities. He could have stayed at the country resort on the other side of town, but figured there was no point as he intended being out and about all weekend.

Zac frowned as the headlights picked up a dark shape ahead and slowed the car as he approached a person walking on the left-hand side of the bitumen road. As he got closer, he could see the high heels and knee length skirt of a woman tramping along in the rain. He almost felt guilty sitting in the warm and dry interior of his BMW. As he drew level with her, he slowed the car to a crawl and pressed the button to take down the electric window on the passenger side.

'Would you like a lift into town? I'm heading there now,' he called out.

She lifted her head and he stared as the familiar voice came through the window.

'Mr Montgomery?'

'Reeza? Is that you?'

As she nodded he stared at the wide-eyed, pale face stuck with damp strands of hair. It was Theresa Anderson, the senior assistant to the executive officer on the international trading floor. She looked like a waif, rather than the best looking, most sophisticated woman on the trading floor. Zac had noticed her the first day she'd started work there a couple of years ago, and over the time he had been very impressed with her dedication to her work. As far as he knew she never socialised with the staff, and never attended the Friday night drinks at Jacksons down the road from the bank. That hadn't stopped him looking for her on the nights he'd gone there with the crowd, but she'd never been there.

He had eventually assumed

that she had a partner she was keen to get home to, and the glimmer of jealousy had surprised him. After that he'd found himself going to that floor more than he'd really needed to, but she had always been professional and not engaged in social chat when he'd tried to start a conversation. Her hands were ring free, not that that meant anything these days.

And not that he'd been looking.

'Quick, jump in. I'll give you a lift.'

'It's okay. It's not far now. I'm too wet to get into your lovely car. I'll ruin the seat.'

Zac drove a short distance past her, pulled to the side of the road and turned the motor off before he got out.

He walked around the back of the car to where Theresa was

standing, took her arm and guided her to the passenger door before she had time to object. 'Don't be silly. Jump in. The leather seats will dry.'

'Are you sure?'

'Of course I am, now hurry up and hop in because I'm getting soaked out here too.'

She quickly climbed into the front seat and Zac shut the door before hurrying around to his side. Once back in the car, he flicked the interior light on and gestured to the glove box.

'There's a box of tissues in there, if you'd like to wipe yourself down a bit. You look miserably wet and cold.'

She opened the glove box and soon there was a small pile of sodden tissues on the floor next to her handbag after she'd dabbed at her hair and face. 'Thank you. I feel a bit more civilised now.'

'I'm assuming you caught a train out here? I passed a railway station a way back. Are you here for the weekend too?' He smiled at her as the thought struck him. 'You're not going to the auction, are you?'

She shook her head. 'No. I don't know about any auction.'

'Ah, that's good then, I'd hate to have to bid against you.' He tried to make her relax with his light-hearted tone. 'Sorry, I'm not sure what to call you. I know your name is Theresa, but I've heard you referred to as Reeza more than that. What shall I call you?'

Even though the light in the car was dim, he noticed her cheeks turn pink.

'Reeza is fine, Mr Montgomery.'

'Zac, please. It's the weekend. There's no need to be formal.'

'What's this auction?' she asked.

'I'm really keen on having a place in the country, and this property ticks all the boxes, so I drove out from the city. If I'd known you were coming this way I could have given you a lift.'

Reeza nodded shyly and gestured outside. 'It's quite pretty out here. When it's not bucketing down, that is. The rain wasn't forecast this far west.'

Zac chuckled. 'If we made as many mistakes with our trading as the weather forecasters do, we'd all be out of a job.'

'I tend to look at the sky and make my own judgement,' she said with a gentle smile. 'Although I did misjudge badly tonight.'

'Why were you walking from the railway station? You weren't getting picked up?'

'Someone from home usually picks me up, but they were madly picking tonight to beat the wind. My dad is picking me up in town in an hour.'

Someone from home? My dad, he wondered? That didn't sound like a partner. And if her dad was picking her up, home must be with family. She must have come out for the weekend.

'You come home on the weekends?'

'No, I live out here.'

Zac stared at her. Even with her makeup washed off, apart from some of that eyelash black stuff under her eyes, Reeza was still a very beautiful woman. 'You mean you do that two hour commute each way every day?' he said, turning his attention back to the car.

'I do. It's good down time.' This time she chuckled. 'Except when it decides to rain, my shoes are sodden, and there's no one waiting for me at the station.'

'So you were walking until you got picked up. Do you live in town?'

'No, out of town. On fifty acres. My family has a stone fruit orchard.'

Zac started the engine and the cosy warmth of the heater surrounded them. Neither of them spoke for a couple of moments as the headlights pierced the darkness ahead. His perception of Theresa Anderson had been way off. She wasn't going home to a partner, she'd been commuting all those months. His interest quickened.

'The turn off to town is about five hundred metres ahead. On the left.' Reeza broke the silence. 'Just drop me anywhere in the main street.' She reached down and picked up her bag from the floor. 'Thank you very much for the lift.'

Zac hesitated. 'You said you had an hour to wait. Would you have dinner with me? I was just going to have a quick meal at a pub. Being a local you might be able to steer me in the right direction.'

'The Federal is the best and quickest meal.'

'Is that a yes to the invitation?' He glanced across at her with a smile.

Chapter 3

For the life of her, Reeza couldn't understand why she'd agreed to have dinner with Zac Montgomery, one of the big bosses from the bank. It had been such a surprise when he'd asked, she hadn't been able to come up with a quick or suitable reason why she couldn't, and anyway, she guessed she had to eat. She couldn't very well show him the Federal Hotel and then sit at a table by herself. Zac was way up the ladder past her, and the word in the bank was that one day he'd take over the top position. He'd always made her nervous when he came to their floor, because he was such a good looking guy, and he had presence. He'd tried to be friendly but she'd put her head down and worked harder whenever he'd come to the floor.

Reeza was used to her father and brothers in their navy blue King Gee work clothes. Zac Montgomery was always beautifully groomed and wore the best suits. His skin was tanned, his hair was jet black, and he had dark blue eyes that a girl could lose herself in. When she'd finally got hold of the remote to the TV last week, she'd binge watched *Poldark*, and as soon as he'd had made his entrance, he had reminded her of Zac Montgomery. A touch of arrogance, and *bucketloads* of sex appeal.

Nervous tingles scurried around inside her as he held the door of the Federal Hotel bistro open for her.

Zac Montgomery having dinner

She wondered if her wet skirt was sticking to her behind, and how damp her white shirt was beneath her jacket. There was no way she was taking it off, despite the pretty lacy underwear that was another of her weaknesses.

The bistro was busy and several locals waved to her, looking curious as Zac led her across to a vacant table near the window.

'That's good, I'll be able to watch for my lift,' she said. He was very polite and went to take her jacket off, but she shook her head. 'Thanks. I'll just slip to the restroom and try to do something with my wet hair.'

'It looks busy here and I know you've only got an hour before your lift, so I'll order while you've gone. What would you like to eat?'

Heat ran into her cheeks this time, and Reeza felt about fifteen again as she stumbled over a coherent response. 'Ah, no . . . um . . . it's okay. Ah, maybe just a salad. Yes, a salad, thanks. A Caesar salad.' Reeza dug in her bag for her purse, but Zac held up his hand and that sexy smile took her breath away.

'We'll sort it later.'

'Thanks. I won't be long.' She turned and looked around when she reached the door of the bistro.

Zac had put his car keys on the table to claim it, and had joined the long queue at the counter. He was taller, better dressed, and *way* better looking than any other man in the room.

Than any other man in the state.

Reeza groaned as she opened the door to the restroom. Heat rushed through her again.

Why was she here with him? What the hell were they going to talk about?

Her mortification was complete when she stood in front of the mirror above the basin. Her hair hung in rats' tails and her mascara had run and was now stuck in clumps below her eyes. Turning to the full length mirror beside the door, she was relieved to see her clothes didn't look too bad. A bit of mud was splashed up the back of her pantihose but she scrubbed that off with her hand before digging into her handbag for her hairbrush.

She grinned at her reflection as she dipped her head beneath the hand dryer and fluffed out her hair before brushing it and securing it in the clip. A dab with a wet tissue to remove the mascara spots, and a quick flick of red lipstick and she looked almost the same as she had when she had left for the office this morning.

Almost.

Certainly not up there with Mr Zac Montgomery.

With straight shoulders and her chin lifted high, she tried to look confident as she slipped her handbag over her shoulder. Reeza pulled a face at her reflection; it didn't work. She looked just as nervous as she felt. It was stupid; this was her town and her home turf, and she'd been having dinner at the Federal Hotel for as long as she could remember. She wasn't at work, and she should be able to consider Zac Montgomery as an acquaintance and not one of the big bosses from work.

A very good looking boss from work.

She swallowed and headed back out to the table. The bistro was even busier, and the local band had started up in the covered beer garden. Children ran around between the tables and she finally relaxed, smothering a grin as she wondered if the family pub atmosphere would turn a city slicker off country life. Maybe it wasn't the bucolic setting that he was imagining. He might think twice about a move out here; Brentwood living was very different to the country life that the glossy magazines and weekend supplements painted of the country west of the city.

Then again, Reeza had never

moved in that set. Maybe they went to the swanky restaurants like the one out at the resort. There probably was a whole life out here that she'd never experienced.

Zac stood as she approached the table and she waved at him to sit down.

'I wasn't sure what you'd like to drink, so I bought a glass of white wine and a soft drink to cover all bases.'

'Thank you. A wine will hit the spot. It's been a very long day.' She glanced at the beer sitting on the table in front of him.

'It has.' Zac leaned back in his chair and looked at her, and she returned his gaze steadily, and decided to take the initiative. Picking up her wine and sipping it, Reeza kept her eyes on his. They were as deep a blue as she'd noticed from a distance over the trading floor, and surrounded by thick dark lashes that were the same colour as his almost jet black hair. 'So a house in the country?' she asked trying to sound interested and sophisticated.

'That's the plan.'

'And I guess it's not for commuting to the city from.'

He lifted his beer and took a sip. 'Who knows? Maybe one day not too far away.'

Reeza nodded. 'Sounds like early retirement.'

'Retirement! I'm not that old.'

He looked most affronted and she smiled. 'I didn't say you were old. Who knows ? You could be planning to start a horse stud, or plant peach trees.' She picked up her wine and took another sip. 'Although I wouldn't recommend the peaches.'

'I've always wanted to live in the country. I grew up in Sydney. Went to uni there, and I've worked there for fifteen years. I can see myself as a gentleman farmer.'

From the tone of his voice, Reeza knew he was teasing her. She chuckled. 'And here am I. I've lived here all my life and it's my dream to live in the city. Right smack bang in the middle where I can see the harbour if I want to and listen to the traffic instead of cows and chooks, and walk to any restaurant. You might think I'm silly, but I've already chosen the colours and the fittings for the day in about twenty years when I can afford my luxury apartment.'

'Nothing like having a plan.' This time Zac smiled and she thought how much younger he looked. 'So you're going to commute until then. That's a lot of train rides.'

She pulled a face and nodded. 'Yep.'

'Next time you're in the city for the weekend let me know.'

She looked at him curiously but he didn't elaborate. 'So tell me about the local area, Reeza. You must know it well.'

'Too well.'

'Have you travelled much?'

She shook her head. 'No. I've been pretty boring. School, uni work. I'm embarrassed to say I've never been out of New South Wales.'

His eyes widened and Reeza found it hard to look away. For the first time she noticed the unusual dark flecks in the blue of his eyes.

'Never?'

Embarrassment flooded her.

Why the hell did I say that?

Pulling herself up straight Reeza looked around, trying to think of another subject apart from how boring her life was. She was no good at this social stuff, especially with someone who was way above her level, professionally and socially.

She was surprised when Zac leaned over and took her hand. 'There's no need to feel as though you're less of a person because you haven't travelled. Let me tell you about my Mum. You'd love her; she is one of the most interesting, well-informed people you'd ever meet. She didn't go to university, and she's never been out of Australia. She still lives in the same house my parents bought at Balgowlah Heights when she married my father. She grew up in a house around the corner from there, and always says why would she go anywhere else?'

'What does she do?' Reeza's interest had been piqued.

'She writes poetry.'

'She sounds interesting. What about your Dad?'

'I don't have a father anymore.' Zac's voice was controlled and his smile disappeared.

'I'm—' Reeza was saved by the loud vibration of the buzzer on the table. She jumped up. 'I'll get the meals. You stay there.'

Before he could answer she'd picked up the buzzer and shot off to the bistro. She glanced at her watch on her way. Forty-five minutes until pick up if Dad was on time. She hoped he'd be running late tonight.

'Hi Reeza. Night out on the town?' Helen, the waitress on the cash register at the bistro smiled at her. They'd gone to school together, and Helen was one of the few who'd stayed local. Reeza had worked in the bistro as a kitchen hand in her first two years at uni, and then graduated to bar work.

'No. Just a late one. Dad's picking me up in in a while.'

'That's a shame. I was checking out the sex on legs you're sitting with. Not a bad looker, love. He looks like that guy in *Poldark*. Where did you find him?'

'He does, doesn't he?' Reeza laughed. 'He's one of my bosses and he gave me a lift in the rain, and then took pity on me and offered me dinner. Which reminds me. How much is the Caesar Salad these days?'

'Twenty-four dollars.' Helen handed over the salad, and a plate holding a huge steak. She winked. 'And here I was thinking he was building up his energy for a big night, and what a lucky girl you were.'

Reeza smiled and shook her head. 'No such luck in my life.' She turned, heated from head to toe as she bumped into Zac who was standing close enough to have heard the entire conversation. A smile played around his mouth and she looked away as he reached for the two plates. 'You get the cutlery, Reeza. I'll take these to the table.'

'Sorry, 'Helen mouthed.

'Shoot me now,' Reza whispered back. She collected two cutlery bags and followed Zac back to the tables. After she'd placed the cutlery on the table, she reached down and pulled out her purse.

'Twenty-four dollars,' she said pushing the right money across towards him. 'For the salad. I'll get us another drink. My shout. What would you like?' She knew she was babbling but she was worried that he'd overheard Helen's comments.

And her reply!

Zac put his hand over hers and pushed it, and the money back to her side of the table. Reeza's mouth dried and she looked down at her hand; it had zinged with an electric shock when he'd touched her fingers.

His eyes were intent on hers when she looked up. 'You don't have to pay me for your dinner, Reeza. I asked you to join me. I've got a favour to ask and that will pay me back anything you think you owe me.'

'A favour?' she said slowly.

'I'd really appreciate if you could spend some time with me tomorrow and show me around the district. That is, unless you have other plans.'

'Um. No. I don't have plans.'

'Excellent. Would you prefer I met you in town or can I pick you up? I'd be interested to see an orchard.'

'If you'd really like to see an orchard you could pick me up.'

Reeza Anderson, what the hell are you doing? She wished she could pull the words right back into the mouth they'd come from.

'We live at Stony Park Orchard. About ten kilometres out on the Thirlmere Road. The orchard name is on the gate. You can't miss it.'

'Good. Say ten?' He tipped his head to the side and his eyes were dancing.

'Ten is fine.'

'Now we'd better eat up. We'll need to build up our energy for our day tomorrow.'

Reeza almost choked on the wine she had just sipped.

Chapter 4
Pentecost Island - Pippa

The music was still thumping, and I shook my head as Rafe tried to pull me up from my chair and take me out to the dance floor again.

'I'm too hot. Go and dance with Cherry. Angus has gone to check on the food. He can't help himself.'

My husband leaned down and kissed me, and gave me a sweet smile before he held his hand out to Cherry and soon they were jiving on the dance floor. Rafe could dance, and he'd confessed to me one day before our wedding that he'd attended weekly dance lessons right through his teens.

He was damn good. I sat there for a minute fanning myself as I let my eyes wander over him. I'd thought he looked like a pirate the first time I'd ever seen him, and tonight he wore one of his long sleeved white silk shirts with the V-neck and the loose ties open at the front.

No shorts and T-shirts for my elegant man. Love for Rafe surged in my chest—so strong it frightened me. I just hoped that I could live up to his expectations, and be the wife he needed.

I left our table and walked across to where Tamsin and Nell were deep in conversation. I smiled as I looked at the two plates laden with food in front of them. 'Private conversation or can anyone join in?'

'Sit down, Pip. We were just talking about you,' Tamsin said

I sat down and looked at them both. 'What did I do?'

They stared at each other and

grinned. 'It's not what you've done,' Nell said.

'Although we hope you have been.' Tamsin's voice was as dry as ever.

Nell chuckled. 'Didn't you notice Rafe and Pippa were late *again*?'

'Have been what?' I said, pretending not to know that I knew exactly what they were talking about.

Nell was the first to break. 'We were wondering how long it'll be before you're pregnant.'

'Or maybe you are already?' Tam's grin was cheeky. 'You've got a real glow about you lately.' She tapped the side of her nose. 'I notice things like that these days.'

'I sure do have a glow. It's called happy.'

Tam and Nell high fived each

other.

'And before your pregnant imaginations run away with you, it's called happiness from full bookings, the staff accommodation being almost finished, the excavator has finished digging the hole for the pool, the concreters are coming and—'

'And?' Nell and Tamsin both leaned forward.

'And my two best friends are going to make me a surrogate aunty twice in the next few months. Sorry gals, I'm not ready yet. Too much is happening here. And I'd like to have some time with my man before I start the nappy and bottle brigade.'

There was no way I was going to let on that Rafe had announced to me six days after our wedding that he was ready to start a family.

Even though I'd told him I was happy, I'd worried about it nonstop ever since. So much, it was keeping me awake at night.

Rafe had noticed I was preoccupied, but I had blamed Ma Carmichael's and the hectic work schedule as we expanded so quickly.

He'd looked at me for a while, and then agreed. 'You work too hard.'

'Not for much longer.' I said. 'The major stuff is underway. And then we can have our honeymoon.'

But he was not easily distracted. 'And our first baby. I'm not getting any younger,' he'd said, 'and I'd like to have fun with our children while I'm still fit enough to give piggyback rides and read nursery rhymes.'

'First?' I'd managed to joke.

'How many do you plan on having?'

He'd grinned and swooped a kiss on my neck. 'At least five.'

I vaguely recall that I had managed a smile and then headed off on the pretext of seeing the Riccardos. I'd taken myself for a long walk to the other side of the island, knowing I should tell him how I was feeling.

But I was too scared to tell him. I didn't want Rafe to stop loving me. I would rather lose everything if it meant Rafe would still love me.

The problem was I didn't know whether I could be a mother. I mean, I'm sure there was no physical reason that I couldn't, I'd never had any problems in the female department, regular as clockwork since the first summer I'd moved here to live with Aunty

Vi.

That first time I'd got my period was such a shock I'd taken myself to bed on the side veranda for the day; I hadn't had a mother to tell me about female things and periods. After a couple of hours Aunty Vi had turned up with a hot water bottle.

'Put that on your tummy, Phillipa. It will ease the cramps and don't worry, they only last for the first day.'

'The first day,' I'd squawked. 'How many days does this go for?'

'Three or four if you're lucky, seven or eight if you're not.'

'God, I want to die,' I'd said dramatically, flinging myself back on the pillow, one hand over my face.

Aunty Vi had stood over me. 'Don't you ever let me hear you

say that again.' She looked down at me for a moment, before brushing the hair back from my forehead, and then she'd turned on her heel and left me alone.

I'd lain back on my bed and looked at the horizontal slats on the old fashioned pull down wooden blinds. One of these horrid things every month from now—I was almost twelve—until I was ancient, about fifty or more. That was almost forty multiplied by twelve months every year. I counted the slats until my eyes blurred and I fell asleep.

I can still remember that day as though it was yesterday. The blinds had gone when we moved back to the island and had been replaced by those horrid thick pull down plastic blinds that kept the weather out. They also kept the view out, so they'd been taken down very quickly when Nell and Tam and I moved into the house.

I'd read the leaflet Aunty Vi gave me. It must have come with the sanitary pads because I couldn't imagine that she would have had it lying around.

But then, Aunty Vi was always full of surprises, and had been well prepared when I'd arrived there when I was eleven. She'd done a good job of getting me through my teens; I'd survived them anyway, and I became a master at hiding the scars that I carried.

Nell and Tam always said I had abandonment issues, but it went a lot deeper than that. Rafe had brought me to a good place, but I'd never told him about the bad times before my mum had taken her own life.

And that was the crux of my problem.

I didn't know if I was capable of being a *good* mother. What if I carried the same problems as my mother had? That same weakness? What if childbirth set me on that same path?

The chances of that happening were pretty good. I had never even told the counsellor my deepest fear.

'Earth to Pippa,' Tam's chuckle interrupted my brooding and I forced a smile to my face, but they both knew me too well. 'Okay, spill, girlfriend. Why the worried face?'

'What were you thinking about then?' Nell asked softly.

This time I worked really hard at the smile. 'You really want to know?

Two nods and intent stares met my gaze.

'I was thinking about the first time I got my period and how Aunty Vi dealt with me.' I chuckled and this time it was half genuine. 'God, I was a drama queen, back then.'

Tam nudged me. 'Back then? You still are!'

'Thanks, I love you too. Be careful if you plan on asking me to babysit. I'll teach your children as many bad habits as I can.' I leaned back in the chair. 'Now are you two going to eat all that food or are you going to share.'

The music and happy voices surrounded me and I managed to smile as I let go of my dark thoughts for a moment.

I had a deeper worry.

Chapter 5

As Reeza stood in front of her open wardrobe in her underwear the following morning she wondered what on earth she'd done accepting an invitation to spend the day showing Zac Montgomery the local district. Not only that, she'd also given him her address to pick her up. The rain must have soaked into her head last night and given her a brain fade.

When she'd seen her father pull up outside the Federal Hotel as she'd been finishing off her salad, she'd jumped up and said a quick goodbye to Zac before Dad could come into the pub.

'See you in the morning,' Zac had said with that sexy smile as she'd fled. What a stupid thing she'd agreed to. His reputation at the bank was that of a lady killer, and she wondered why on earth he'd asked her to come with him tomorrow, although to be honest, there'd been no sign of a lady killer—apart from the blue eyes and the sexy smile— he had been very polite and reserved over dinner. Plus it *had* been kind of him to offer her a lift in the rain. He could have sailed straight past her last night.

Today was probably because he wanted directions to get around. Um, no, he would have a Sat Nav, she told herself.

Maybe he thought she'd know of other properties for sale. Anyway, Zac insisted that he was very interested in the one up for auction out near the Oaks. Shite, he was picking her up in fifteen minutes and she still hadn't decided what to wear.

She stood at the open door of her old wooden wardrobe and stared at the selection. Three black, and two navy-blue suits that she rotated for work, and six white shirts. At the far end were three dresses she'd had for years. Two of them had been bought for friends' weddings, and the other was the dress she'd worn to her twenty-first birthday party. Buying clothes meant she paid less of her uni debt, and added time to when she could move to the city. For the first time Teresa regretted her lack of clothes.

On the shelf above the hanging space were shorts and T-shirts she wore in the orchard, and one good pair of jeans.

So the choice was the jeans

and a white shirt from work, or the twenty-first party dress.

She stood there tapping one finger on her lips, aware that the minutes were scooting by.

Okay, it was warm enough for a dress. The rain had cleared overnight, and the southerly had dropped. Reeza grabbed the blue and white floral dress from the hanger and slipped it over her underwear. She knew she had a pair of matching sandals somewhere. Scrabbling around in the bottom of her wardrobe gave no success, and another five minutes passed before she finally found the blue and white shoes, covered in mould, in a box in the laundry.

It took a few minutes to wipe the mould off with a damp rag and she threw the shoes into the clothes dryer for five minutes, the banging of the shoes in the drum thumping through the house as she hurried to the bathroom to do something with her face and hair.

'Shite, shite, shite,' Reeza muttered three minutes before ten. Hopefully, Zac would be late. She raced into the bathroom she shared with her brothers and groaned when she opened the drawer. Someone had tidied it; her hairbrush and clips had all disappeared. Even the one she'd put on the side of the sink last night wasn't there anymore.

As she pulled open the other drawers Reeza groaned as she saw two boxes of condoms. One day she would have her own apartment and not have to share with her brothers.

Gawd, if she even needed

condoms—not that there was any chance of that—she'd know where to look now. But a hair clip? Not a blasted one in sight.

When she had her own unit, everything would be in its place and she'd have time to get ready in a leisurely manner.

And have nice things at her fingertips, where she put them, and where no one interfered with them.

As she slammed the drawer shut, the front doorbell rang. Grabbing a comb from the shelf she ran it through her hair, fluffed it up and left it loose.

No time.

Grabbing her lipstick off the hallstand, she hurried towards the front door. At least there was no one else home. Her parents and both her brothers had headed out straight after breakfast. Dad had glared at her when he'd told her she was pruning the back half of the house paddock this morning, and she'd shaken her head.

'Sorry, I have plans,' she said.

Lyle had added his glare, and his mouth, to the disapproval around the table.

'Jeez, Reez, that makes more work for Ted and I.'

Ted, God love him, flashed her a sympathetic look. He was her favourite brother. Lyle was just like Dad.

'Well, I'm sorry, but I do have a life outside the orchard,' she said crossly. 'And I have been at work all week.'

'That's your choice,' Dad muttered.

Reeza had rolled her eyes, and Mum called out as she went down the hall. 'Can you do the chooks for me this morning, please, love? I have to go into town again. It's my morning on the CWA stall and with the two auctions on, there'll be a crowd in town for morning tea.'

Feeding the chooks and collecting six dozen eggs had made Reeza even later, and by the time she came back to the house, she'd needed another shower and her hair got wet again.

Maybe it would be worth the extra expense to move out now, she thought as she hurried to the front door. Life at the bank was a breeze compared to a weekend at home.

Opening the front door, she pulled it hard because it always stuck, but someone had obviously greased the lock and the door almost knocked her off her feet before slamming into the wall with a loud bang that echoed down the hall.

Heat ran into her cheeks as she looked into Zac Montgomery's amused eyes.

'I'm delighted by your enthusiasm to see me,' he said with a cheeky grin.

God, now he even sounded like Ross Poldark.

'Someone oiled the catch,' she said in her defence, trying not to stare at the gorgeous man standing on the doorstep.

'And I thought it was me.' He gestured to the car parked in the circular drive. 'Your chariot awaits, madame.'

'I just have to get my bag. Oh, and my shoes. Have a wander around and look at Mum's roses. They're her pride and joy.'

Before he had a chance to agree or disagree, Reeza ran to collect her shoes from the clothes dryer, and find her bag that she hadn't seen anywhere this morning,

Damn. The sole on each shoe had come away and it was sticky beneath her feet. With a grimace, she pulled both shoes on. She'd just have to ignore the stickiness all day.

Not a good start.

She'd left her handbag in the living room last night, and of course Mum had put it away somewhere when she'd tidied up this morning.

Their mother drove them all crazy with her tidiness. The only problem was she would get side-tracked and put things in the strangest places. It was another five minutes before Reeza found her handbag in the pantry next to the spare egg cartons. Grabbing a handful of tissues from the top of the fridge, she shoved them in her bag, checked her purse was in there, and ran for the front door, grabbing her lipstick off the hallstand on the way past. She still hadn't put any on.

Zac was waiting by his car.

'Sorry,' she said. 'You wouldn't believe my life here. I change universes when I get off the train every day, I'm sure.'

'No problem. Don't stress. We have plenty of time. I thought a coffee in town first?'

'That would be good.' Zac held the door open for her and she looked up at him. 'At least I'm dry today.'

'And looking very lovely, might

I say' he said. 'I'm used to the corporate Ms Anderson with the pulled back hair and the black suit.'

Reeza smiled. 'You're looking very casual too, Mr Montgomery. I'm used to the navy blue suit and the ties, and the artfully styled hair.'

Shite. Did I actually say that?

'That's my work look. This is the real me,' he said. 'Sometimes I wonder why I ever went into the business world.'

Reeza settled into the car as he walked around the front and settled into the driver's seat. She'd always found Mr Mont—Zac—friendly and polite in the office, but this was a new lighter side she was seeing today.

And she liked it.

She liked him. Boyish and relaxed.

Letting out a breath, Reeza decided she could relax too. It was Saturday. The sun was shining, they were away from the bank, and she had no one to impress.

'It's a great day. Would it mess with your hair if I put the top down?' Zac asked.

'Not at all, I should have a hair band in here somewhere.' She dug in her bag and was in luck for the first time this morning. She pulled out a blue scrunchie to match her dress and her hair was restrained in seconds. 'I'd love it. It's on my bucket list to ride in a sports car with the top down.

'I'm impressed,' he said. 'No fuss, no bother with your hair.'

'That's the me I would like to be,' she said with a rueful smile. 'But living at home does not lend itself to being organised.'

'I know what you mean. I'm embarrassed to admit to it, but would you believe I'm living back in the family home where I grew up?'

'Really?' Her smile widened. 'I don't feel so old-fashioned when I hear that.'

Zac pressed a button and when the soft top had slid down silently, he started the engine. 'It's not old-fashioned. It's the new way. So many thirty somethings still live at home with their parents these days.' He chuckled. 'I invited Mum to come with me last night, but she was horrified.'

'Horrified?' Reeza stretched her legs out in the generous space in the front of the car. 'Why horrified?'

'Horrified that a man of my age was asking his mother to go with him. I get the regular "when are you going to get married and give me grandchildren?" talk. But it's getting a bit too frequent for comfort now. So I'm looking for my own place.'

'How old are you?' She slid a sideways glance at him, wondering if that was the right thing to ask.

'I'll be thirty-seven next birthday.'

'Never married?' she asked, feeling very game.

'No. Went close once, but I managed to escape.'

Reeza chuckled because it seemed to be the response he wanted.

Zac turned the sports car to the right onto the main road, and she crossed her fingers hoping that Dad and the boys wouldn't be in the front paddock near the road.

No such luck. As the sports car gathered speed, she spotted Dad up a ladder in the front of the orchard, and Lyle and Ted at the fence taking a break. Lyle pointed to the car and Ted turned around, and then both her brothers' eyes widened when they saw her sitting in the front seat.

'I'll cop some teasing about that tonight,' she said, pulling a face. 'Honestly, it's like being fifteen-years-old still. Sorry, you don't want to hear my woes.' Embarrassment flooded through her as Reeza realised how gauche she must seem. If Zac had been with one of the women she'd seen with him in the social pages—yes, she had taken note—they'd probably be talking about overseas trips, or skiing in Aspen, or the state of the stock market.

A light bulb came on in her head.

I can do that.

'Did you see the All Ordinaries was up this morning?' she said turning to him.

He looked at her curiously. 'No.'

'Oh.'

'I'd rather hear about your family, and your life out here. Is that all they do? I mean is the farm a working farm? Not a hobby for your family?' Zac changed back a gear as they zoomed up the last hill before town.

'Yes. It's a working farm and I'm the black sheep of the family because I went to uni and got a real job. Dad would much rather have me at home in the packing shed all day.'

'If you had done that, it would

have been a loss for the bank. You're very good at your job, Reeza.'

Oh wow.

She looked away at the peach trees flashing past so he didn't see the smile that lifted her lips. 'Thank you. I do enjoy it,' she said quietly. 'Now enough about me. Tell me what we're doing today and where this property is.'

Chapter 6

Zac stilled as attraction slammed into him. Reeza had put her head back and laughed when the tiny teacup almost slipped from his fingers, but he caught it before any tea spilled. She'd relaxed after a half hour of sitting in the garden at the back of a quaint coffee shop that she'd insisted was the best in town.

'What?' He grinned. 'A man is allowed to love his cup of tea.'

'I know, but it was seeing you trying to put your finger through that handle that tickled me. Look, this is how you do it.' Her fingers brushed his as she reached across and took his teacup, holding the fine gold handle between her thumb and two fingers. 'See?'

He nodded gravely. 'You

obviously have more experience than me in the art of tea drinking. I usually have mine in a mug.'

'Philistine,' she said. Reeza's smile was wide and her eyes were dancing.

After she'd put his cup back on the saucer, Zac reached over and took her fingers before she could pull away. Her pretty green eyes met his. 'It's good to see you finally relax. You have a lovely smile.'

'Thank you. I'm feeling good. It's Saturday, the sun is shining, and we have a fun day ahead. I've never been to an auction before. And you know what the best thing of all is?'

'Me?' He quirked an eyebrow and tried to look hopeful, but it didn't work because she chuckled again.

Reeza put her other hand to her chest. 'I'm sorry. I'm acting like a fourteen-year-old. I'll be serious now.' She composed her face into an expression more like the one she wore at work, and two tiny frown lines appeared on her forehead, but her eyes still held his.

Zac realised her hand was still in his, but she seemed comfortable. 'No. I much prefer the giggling Reeza. And if I'm not the best thing of all, what is? Or should I ask who is?'

She leaned forward and spoke quietly. 'The best thing is you got me out of pruning peach trees.'

Zac let go of her hand and focused on lifting the tiny cup. 'You still work in the orchard too?'

She nodded glumly. 'Yep, it's a family concern, and the family is expected to pitch in. I can't complain because my brothers work a seven day week.'

'Still, you must find it hard after a week at the bank, and that huge commute every day.'

Reeza dropped her eyes from his. 'I guess I feel guilty and I'm trying to make up to Dad for going to uni and getting a job in town..'

'Your steel trap mind would be a whiz with the financial records of the orchard.' Zac had seen a lot of her work at the bank and she was one very smart economist.

She shook her head. 'No, that's his domain. I just get to do the outside work with the boys. But enough about me. I've got the day off, and I'm going to make the most of it, so tell me about this property, and why you would want to move here from the city.' She tipped her head to the side as though it was hard to believe that he was really interested in moving out to the country.

Zac marshalled his thoughts and looked past her. Her eyes were distracting him every time he looked at her. They were an unusual shade of green with flecks of gold and fringed by dark eyelashes that he was pretty sure were natural. Her skin was flawless and as far as he could tell she wasn't wearing makeup. 'I want to have something of my own, with lots of space around me, where I can relax and be away from the crowds in the city. To start with it'll just be for weekends, but when I leave the bank, it will be my home.'

Her eyes met his again, and that strange jolt ran along his

nerve endings. 'By yourself?'

He nodded. 'Yes, at this stage. I'm happy in my own company, and there's no one in my life that I want to live with. 'He lowered his voice and smiled. 'But if you ever meet my mother, please don't repeat that.'

He frowned as her voice rose and she looked over his shoulder.

'Oh, no.' Her eyes widened and she picked her cup up and then put her head down. 'Brace yourself,' she whispered.

Before Zac could turn around, a firm hand settled on his shoulder.

'Well, well, hello there. Aren't you a dark horse, Theresa Anderson? When were you going to tell us you've got yourself a man? No wonder you wouldn't help Dad today.'

Zac looked up into eyes that

were the same colour as Reeza's. Before he could speak, she replied to the woman he assumed was her mother. Apart from the eyes there was absolutely no other resemblance. Even though it wasn't raining, for some reason this buxom, ruddy-cheeked woman was wearing a yellow raincoat, and a rain hat inside.

'Mum, please. This is Mr Montgomery, my *boss* from work. I'm helping him with a business transaction this weekend. Mr Montgomery, this is my mother, Heather.'

'Oh.' The word was laced with disappointment. 'So it's work, is it?'

Zac put the teacup down and held his hand out. 'How do you do, Mrs Anderson. It's a pleasure to meet you. I'm sorry I took your daughter away from her work at the orchard, but I needed assistance today, and I couldn't expect her to come all the way into town.'

Her mother nodded, and lifted her hand. 'That's a shame, but at least if you get home early enough, Reez, you can still help Dad and the boys.'

Zac frowned wondering what the "that's a shame" referred to.

'I'll see,' Reeza replied.

'Did you do the chooks?'

She nodded and her expression was bland. 'Yes, there were six dozen eggs.'

'Good,' her mother said briskly, and nodded at Zac. 'Try not to keep her out too long, will you, mate?'

'Mum?' Reeza frowned at her mother. 'Why are you wearing a raincoat and that crazy hat?

Her mother's laugh was rich and warm. 'While the girls were manning the cake stall, I cleaned out the fridge in the CWA rooms. I didn't want to get my good dress dirty.'

Reeza's eyes lit up. 'Um, and the hat?'

'Oh, my stars! It fell out of my pocket when I was in the fridge, and I put it on so I wouldn't lose it. I forgot I had it on. How embarrassing. You'll think I'm a complete country yokel, Mr Montgomery.' Her ruddy cheeks deepened to a burnished red. Taking the hat off and stuffing it into her pocket, her eyes met Zac's and she grinned. 'Please don't judge my sweet daughter by her silly mum, will you? We're nothing alike.' She turned and went to the counter, and Zac and Reeza sat there without speaking until she'd collected her takeaway coffee and strode from the shop.

Reeza's head was down and her shoulders were shaking. Her hand was clenched on top of the table and Zac put his on top of it. And he thought he had problems with his mother telling him what to do.

'God, I'm sorry if I made things really hard for you. You should have—'

He stopped as Reeza lifted her head and he looked into a pair of dancing eyes and a wicked grin. '"Try not to keep me out too long, mate?" I've a good mind to stay out in the sticks the whole weekend. And did I feed the chooks! Of course I fed the bloody chooks. I do every morning. Honestly, if I didn't laugh, I'd—'

She chuckled again.

'I thought you were crying,' he said quietly.

'God no. Laughing's the only way you can survive in our household. Otherwise I'd be as crazy as my mad family. They're okay. Mum's a sweetheart. She always has a cause and is running around looking after someone in need.' Reeza picked up her cup and sipped. 'But you know what? I am, you know.'

'You are what?'

'Like Mum. The Reeza you see at the bank is on her best behaviour. I'm afraid I inherited Mum's habit of telling it how it is. I've learned to control my tongue in the hallowed halls of the bank.'

'I can deal with that. I admire honesty. I just have one request.'

Her eyes met his again and

those blasted nerves skittered around. 'What would that be?'

'No yellow rain hats.'

'I think I can do that for today.' Her smile was sweet. 'Although I could have done with one last night.'

Zac leaned forward. 'Have I created an inconvenience for the whole family by asking you out today?' He hadn't been able to resist her. And he had taken a while to get to sleep last night as he couldn't get Reeza out of his mind. While her local knowledge was handy, it was the thought of spending the day in her company that had prompted his invitation at dinner last night.

'No, you haven't. I'm a big girl now. I don't have to ask permission, even if Dad doesn't like it. Come on, let's get out of here before Mum's curiosity gets the better of her and she comes back.'

Zac jumped up and waited as Reeza stood and lifted her bag off the spare chair.

'Welcome to the country,' she said. 'My country. I think it's a bit different to your genteel expectations.'

Chapter 7

The day in the sticks—as Reeza had called it after Mum's country bumpkin performance—went way too fast. She enjoyed watching the auction, even though Zac didn't bid because he said the property wasn't as good as he'd thought it would be.

The crowd bidding were all out of the city. There wasn't one local face; even the real estate agent was from Sydney. When the auctioneer's hammer came down at 2.4 million dollars, Reeza stood there staring at Zac, her mouth open in disbelief.

'Who on earth would pay that for a scrappy bit of land and a house that needs a motza spent on it? And the orchard needs chopping out.'

'You'd be surprised.'

'Stunned is a better word.' As they walked back to the car, she turned to Zac. 'I can't believe anyone would pay that sort of money for any house and land.'

He looked at her curiously. 'With the transactions you handle every day, you must realise how much is spent on real estate internationally. The local market is the same.'

'I guess. It makes me think I'll never be able to afford the apartment I'm saving for.' As they reached the car, she paused. 'Anyway, it's been a lovely day. Thank you for asking me. I've had fun.'

'It's not over yet,' Zac said as he opened the passenger door.

'Aren't you driving back to the city now?'

'No, I booked the motel for another night. I'm going to have a bit more of a look around. I was hoping you'd come with me this afternoon and . . .' Reeza waited as he hesitated.

'And?'

'And have dinner with me tonight.'

'At the pub again?'

'No. I'd like to check out the restaurant at that country resort we passed.' Zac reached for her hand. 'Please? I'll be lonely by myself.'

'This is the man who told me he doesn't mind being by himself. Yes, I'll have dinner with you, but do you know how exxie it is?'

'Exxie?'

'Expensive.'

'Ah. Not an economic term I'm familiar with.' He grinned down at her, and that warm feeling that had tugged at her all day came rushing back.

'Well, you need to broaden your vocabulary,' she said. 'And if you want to go there for dinner, I'd say you'll have to book.'

'Is that a yes?'

Reeza hesitated, as the contents of her wardrobe filled her thoughts. 'Do you think it would be pretty posh? I mean, what should I wear?'

Zac shook his head. 'Something like you're wearing now will be fine. I'm not dressing up. I wear a suit all week. I'll just change my shirt. If you want to get changed, I can drop you home and pick you up later.'

Reeza weighed up the choices. Her oldest bridesmaid dress was a red sheath, and not too dressy.

Formal would have been good; she adored the other dress. Go as she was, or go home and change into the red one and risk Zac encountering Mum again, or even worse, Dad.

'Okay, I'll get changed at home later, if you're happy to wait for me.'

He held her eyes with his. 'Of course I, am. Ah, will your mother be there?'

'Probably.' Reeza laughed as she got into the car. 'Why? Are you scared of her?

She couldn't stop laughing when Zac nodded. 'I think so.'

Chapter 8

Zac looked out over the orchard as he sat on the side veranda of Reeza's family home. He'd been relieved when they'd pulled up and there'd been no one else there.

'Looks like the pruning all got done,' she said. 'Dad and the boys will be down at the pub having a bet.'

She'd led him through the old farmhouse to the kitchen and made him a coffee, and then settled him on the veranda while she changed for dinner.

A table was booked at the Country Pines Resort for six-thirty. When he'd made the booking, Zac had raised his eyebrows when he'd been told that the dress was formal.

'Just one moment, please.' He'd put his hand over the phone. 'You were right, It is formal, Is that a problem?'

Reeza shook her head. 'No. I've got something suitable at home.'

He'd booked early for six-thirty in the bar and seven to be seated for dinner. Zac was starving, they'd only had a light lunch before they'd gone to the auction and then gone for a long drive around the district for a few hours, and didn't pass one coffee shop the whole time.

He sat outside sipping a coffee—instant—and looked out over the orchard. Daylight saving hadn't ended yet, and the sun was hovering over the horizon now. It was a pretty sight, the orchards back lit by the golden sun. Even though the farmhouse here was old, the land was prime. The fruit trees that hadn't been pruned looked lush and healthy. There were a couple of boxes of peaches and apricots on a table near where he was sitting, and he'd never seen such plump, healthy fruit in the supermarket.

If he could find land like this, he'd retire and become a gentleman farmer, He'd done well in the fifteen years he'd worked for the international bank, and his investments were solid.

There was also the inheritance from his father that he refused to touch, much to Mum's displeasure.

'I don't understand you, Zac. Tell me honestly. You don't enjoy working at the bank anymore, do you?'

'Not really.'

'You have no commitments, no

one to tie you down. You should be off travelling and experiencing life. I worry about you, darling. Promise me, you'll think about it.'

'Okay,' he'd said. 'I promise to think about it.'

And he had. Here he was looking at land, and planning his exit from the bank. Zac stood and put the mug on the table and wandered over to the railing. He smiled, a dozen chickens were picking around the grass, and the low moo of a cow drifted up the valley. There was no sound of traffic, no voices.

Just blissful quiet. He could get used to this very quickly. The toxic atmosphere in the bank had been pissing him off lately, and he was unimpressed with the new CEO. Getting a call at home at eleven p.m. and having to find files and print and bind them, and then deliver them to the CEO's house at Double Bay in time for a nine a.m. meeting was becoming a too frequent occurrence. He was smart enough to know that it was Drummond trying to exert his authority.

'Confidential, Montgomery,' he would say. 'I can't trust those figures with anyone else.'

It made Zac feel like a glorified secretary, rather than the head of the trading floor. Some of the deals and meetings over the past three months had made him feel uncomfortable. There was an execution mentality if analysts didn't deliver. They had lost a lot of staff in the short time since Drummond had taken over, and he knew he wasn't going to be far behind.

But Zac would go by choice. When he was ready.

'I'm ready.' A soft voice interrupted his brooding and echoed his thoughts.

His breath caught in his throat as he swung around, and his heart began to thud. Reeza stood there looking like . . . looking like something he'd never seen before. Her blue and silver dress clung to her body like a second skin. It was low cut in a straight line and the sleeves began at the top of her arms, leaving both shoulders bare.

Finally, he managed to speak. 'Wow.'

Her face coloured pink and she frowned. 'Is it a bit overdone?'

'No, it's perfect.'

'And my shoes don't match.' She held out one foot to show him the same blue shoes he'd noticed her wearing today.

'Trust me.' He walked over and stood beside her and was enveloped in a sweet floral fragrance. 'No one is going to be looking at your shoes. You look amazing.'

Her cheeks were even pinker. 'Thank you. I was a bridesmaid a few years ago, and I haven't worn it since.'

'I feel sorry for the bride. Nothing could match that dress.'

'There were six of us, but Natalie looked stunning.'

'Let's go.' Zac reached for her hand and was pleased when she didn't hesitate to curl her hand in is. 'I've got a couple of quick stops to make on our way.'

Chapter 9

Zac was quiet as they drove back through town and Reeza wondered if he'd regretted asking her for dinner. He put the indicator on and turned into the car park of the local motel.

'First stop. I'll be quick. Just wait there.'

While she was waiting, she slipped her shoes off and scrubbed at the soles with a tissue, but all it did was stick bits of tissue to the shoe beneath her feet. The stickiness had been driving her crazy all day. Last time she'd ever put shoes in the clothes dryer. She could have worn her high black work shoes, but she was sure they weren't going to recover from the drenching they got last night. At least in the restaurant she could hopefully slip the sticky sandals off under the table.

The door of Zac's motel room closed behind him and Reeza quickly slipped her shoes back on as he walked over to the car. She smiled when he got into the car.

'Wow,' she said. 'Nice suit.'

He pulled a face as he started the car. 'It's not, you know. It's the one I wore to work yesterday and was still wearing when I encountered the waif in the rain last night.'

'Looks as good as new to me, and you know, you didn't have to pick me up.'

Zac's voice was low and sent a shiver down her spine. 'I am very pleased I did.

The shiver was replaced by warmth that went from her toes to her head. 'Anyway,' she said casually, 'we both look the part, so let's go and try this posh restaurant. I'm starving!'

'Me too.' His eyes lingered on her face before he turned the car towards the road.

##

An hour later, they'd had a couple of predinner drinks in the bar of the poshest place that Reeza had ever been in, and the maître 'd came to escort them to their table.

She kept her voice low. 'I had no idea there was anything like this near Brentwood. It's way out of my usual scene.' She moved closer so Zac could hear her low words and was surprised at his reply when he leaned closer.

'It's way out of my usual scene too.'

'I thought you'd be out most weekends.'

'I am, but nothing to compare to this.' His breath brushed her cheek as she leaned closer. 'I spend a lot of time on the harbour. I love being on the water.'

Once they were settled at their table by the window, the maître 'd filled their water glasses and directed their attention to the menus that were at the side of each setting. 'I shall return with the wine list, sir. There doesn't appear to be one on your table. I am very sorry.'

Zac waved a casual hand. 'No worries.'

Reeza looked through the panoramic window at the rolling hills dotted with sheep. The early evening set a rosy glow on the trees and ethereal light hit the top of the hill in shafts of gold. 'And you want to move to the bush?

When it looks like this it really is appealing. It's not how it is you know, in drought and storm, and isolation from all the facilities in the city,'

He pulled a face. 'I want to move to the country.'

'Uh uh.' Reeza shook her head. 'It's the bush. I haven't been there, but I've seen the photos. You're not in the Cotswolds here.'

Zac held her gaze intently. 'You're right you know. Maybe I'm following a dream I really don't want.'

'Especially if you love the water. The best we can offer is the water storage reservoir at the back of the Oaks.' She tipped her head to the side and held those blue eyes with hers. 'If you could do anything you wanted, and money and time and people didn't matter, what would you do?'

'That's easy. I'd have a big luxury boat and travel around the world.'

'Sounds pretty good to me.' Reeza chuckled and earned a glimmer of a smile from the maître 'd as he glided to the table and handed the wine list to Zac.

'Is this table suitable for sir's requirements?'

Zac nodded. 'It is excellent, thank you, Raoul.' He read the name off the badge pinned to the man's white shirt.

Raoul reached for the white linen napkin in the circular crystal holder in front of Reeza and placed it carefully on her lap before he did the same for Zac. 'If you choose the degustation menu, sir, the wine is included with the meal.'

'Thank you, we'll have a look.'

Zac held up his hand as Raoul went to move away. 'Raoul, may I ask you if there is a taxi service from here to town?'

The man frowned and shook his head. 'No, sir. Are you not an in-house guest?'

'No. We drove out from town.'

He shook his head mournfully as though someone had died in his restaurant. 'Well then, sir, the only thing I can suggest if you would like to have wine tonight is that you book a room. I believe there is a vacancy.'

'Thank you. If you could leave the menus and the wine list, and give us ten minutes that would be excellent.'

Reeza opened her menu and her eyes went straight to the prices. She'd intended having the cheapest meal, but she frowned;

there were no prices listed.

Zac looked over the top of his menu as she closed hers and laid it on the table. 'Problem?' he asked.

Reeza shook her head. 'It's in French.'

'My favourite food,' he said with a smile. 'All those garlic cream sauces. To die for.' He put his menu down and leaned forward. 'I do fancy the look of the degustation option, and there is a different wine with each of the courses. Seems a shame to miss out on it, just because there's no taxi service. Please don't take this the wrong way, but what do you think if I book a suite. A *two* bedroom suite.'

Reeza decided to play this in a sophisticated manner, although her legs had gone to jelly when Zac mentioned booking a room. 'I think that sounds like a sensible idea. The only other alternative would be to get someone from home to come out and pick us up.' She shook her head. 'But it's too far, and I'd never hear the end of it.' She stifled a giggle. 'And I can't see you in Dad's work ute.'

'Oh no, don't do that. If there's no suite, we'll have a simple meal, share a bottle of wine and an early night. But we will come back out here when we can try the degustation menu. Apparently they only offer it once a month.'

Excitement zinged along Reeza's nerves. It sounded like he wanted to see her again. She looked up as Raoul appeared beside Zac.

'Ah, Raoul. We would like to have the degustation menu, but before we decide, could you please check the availability of a suite for the evening.'

'Certainly, sir.'

Reeza sat there biting her lip, recalling the balance of her working account and wondering how much this was going to cost. Because there was no way she was going to let Zac pay for dinner and the accommodation. She could afford it, but she'd have to transfer some funds across with her phone.

There was also no way she was going to end the night early and go back to a house where the TV would be blaring, and smart comments would be made about her dress, and her having a date. Her face heated as he stared at her intently.

'You look worried. If you'd like to have the simple menu and an early night, just say it. I won't mind at all. We can come back next month.'

'I'm happy to stay. I'd like to stay. We're all dolled up and sitting in a beautiful restaurant. And you saw how hard it is to get a taxi around here. I very much doubt that the one local taxi would drive out this far.' She swallowed and her cheeks warmed as she held his eyes and spoke honestly. 'I did like hearing you say we could come back another time.'

Zac reached over and took her hand. 'I've enjoyed spending time with you, Reeza. I've really enjoyed today, and I'd like to do it again.'

'Me too,' she said shyly. 'But what about work? It will cause talk. You know the problem with favouritism and all that. Seeing the boss is not a good idea.' Her face flamed as he frowned and she wondered if she'd said too much. Maybe he'd only wanted company to go out, not "seeing", but Zac's next words filled her with relief.

'What we do on the weekends and at night has nothing to do with the bank. I want to get to know you, and I hope you feel the same way. I find your honesty refreshing, Reeza.'

Raoul came back to the table and handed a bill fold to Zac. 'You are in luck, sir. We are able to accommodate you.'

'Thank you, Raoul.'

'If you could note your details in the folder, and slip your credit card in, I'll get it organised for you over at reception.'

Zac did as requested and sat back. 'Would you like me to read the menu to you?'

Reeza was excited, but still trying to look as though she did this on a regular basis. She didn't get out much, and she was going to savour every minute of the night and the new experience.

Oh shite! she thought. If she was going to go out with him again, she'd have to go clothes shopping. And shoe shopping. In one day Zac had seen two of the three dresses in her wardrobe and he was very familiar with the corporate suits and white shirts she wore to work each day.

Reeza blinked as she realised he was staring at her again, but this time a smile tipped his lips. 'Sorry, I was miles away,' she said,

The main lights had dimmed as the restaurant had filled up, and Raoul lit the two long tapers on their table.

'You have the most expressive face, Reeza. It's not going to stand you in good stead if you want to promote to a trading role.'

She grinned at him. 'Okay, let's see how good you are. Tell me what I was thinking.'

'You were wondering if you made the right choice. You were thinking how hungry you are, and how tempting the menu is, not to mention the attentive partner you have tonight.' His thumb rubbed the skin on the back of her hand. 'I hope you weren't worrying if you've made the right choice or not.'

'Shall I tell you how far off the mark you are?'

'Am I?' He pulled a mock pout. 'You were thinking of ringing your dad to pick us up so you could get away from your boring boss.'

'I was thinking about shoes.'

'Shoes?' She was getting used to that sexy grin.

'Uh huh.' She nodded. 'Yes, shoes.'

Chapter 10

Reeza leaned back in her chair and pushed her dessert plate away. Zac grinned at her as he had been all night, and she had relaxed in his company as each of the nine courses had been served.

'My God,' she said. 'I don't think I'll need to eat until next weekend. I thought a degustation menu was supposed to be small portions!'

Zac picked up the course list that Raoul had placed on the table when they had indicated that they would go for the degustation choice. As he read, his deep voice sent a warm shiver down Reeza's spine.

'Degustation at our fine restaurant is a slow appreciative tasting of our local produce food, focusing on the senses, high culinary art and good company. We hope you will enjoy sampling the *small* portions of all of our chef's signature dishes.'

'I certainly enjoyed every mouthful. But they weren't small.'

Zac leaned over and touched the corner of her lips with his thumb. 'You missed a little bit of apricot mousse.'

'Oh how embarrassing. You can't take me anywhere.' Reeza picked up her napkin and dabbed at her mouth.

'I enjoyed watching you eat. It's good to see a woman with an appetite.' He dropped his eyes back to the menu. 'Look. There's your orchard. Peaches and apricots supplied by our local Stony Park Orchard.'

'Wow. I didn't know that.'

Reeza pulled a face. 'But then again, I don't have much to do with the business. Dad pretty much wiped me when I told him I was going to uni. They weren't impressed with my choice of career.'

'I'm pleased you made that choice. I wouldn't have met you if you hadn't.'

She looked up as Raoul hovered at the side of their table and held up a bottle of liqueur. 'The final drink on the menu tonight is our peach brandy. May I tempt you both? Just a taste.'

Reeza blinked. She'd been feeling warm and fuzzy since the small glass of red they'd sampled with the local lamb, and she knew that had a lot to do with how much she'd relaxed. Holding up her glass, she nodded. 'Just a taste, thank you, Raoul.'

The maître 'de smiled and half-filled the small liqueur glass. 'Sip it slowly, madam. It's quite potent.'

Zac held her eyes as she picked up the glass and sipped. The liqueur fizzed on her tongue and warmed her throat on the way down.

His smile was lazy as she blinked. 'Good?'

'Excellent,' she said, but her tongue felt thick and it was hard to pronounce the word. 'But I think one sip will do me.'

Zac sipped his peach brandy slowly until the glass was empty. 'Thank you for your company. I haven't enjoyed a meal as much for a long time. Are you right to leave?'

Reeza was feeling mellow and the nervousness that had gripped her earlier about sharing a suite with Zac had disappeared.

'I am.'

'I was going to suggest a walk around the grounds to walk off some of that food. Or would you prefer to go straight to bed?'

Heat zinged through Reeza's blood. It had been a long time since she had spent a night with man. Not since she and Jai, a fellow student, had gone out for a while in third year uni. She wasn't sure what Zac's expectations were, so she would tread carefully.

'A walk is a good idea,' she said softly.

Zac stood and came around behind her and took her hand as she rose. As they walked to the door he paused at the counter. 'Please charge the meals to my room, Raoul. Thank you for a fine evening.'

'Thank you, Raoul.' Reeza echoed. The night had been a whole new experience for her, and she'd felt very well looked after. Growing up on a farm where every dollar was watched, and then being a uni student, had meant any nights out had been at pubs and bistros. She turned to Zac as they reached the main door of the building. 'And thank you, Zac, for suggesting coming here. It was amazing.' She hesitated and bit her lips wondering how to bring up sharing the bill. 'Um, I would be much more comfortable splitting the bill when we check out tomorrow.'

He shook his head immediately. 'No, this was my idea, and I invited you out.'

'But the room, the cost—' she

said.

'Reeza, please.' He held her hand as they walked down the steps to the circular drive that was edged by a rose garden. The smell of the blossoms filled the night air. 'I insist, and I can afford it, if that bothers you.'

'Okay, well I insist that you let me take you to a place I love in Oxford Street one night, and that will be my shout.'

'Okay, we'll see.' Zac tucked her hand into the crook of his arm and they stepped off the drive and followed a path through the gardens. 'Are you warm enough?'

'Yes, I'm still glowing from all that food and wine,' she said with a chuckle.

They were quiet as they walked through the magnificent gardens. The late summer blooms were almost done but the smell of lavender and roses surrounded them as they trod on the petals littering the path. As they turned to come back around to the building, Zac let go of her hand and turned to face her. His hands were warm on each side of her waist as he lowered his head, and a thrill of anticipation sent a flutter though her lower belly. Reeza closed her eyes as his lips gently brushed hers in a butterfly kiss. Her hands crept up and she slipped her arms around his neck, and Zac's lips were warm on hers as he deepened the kiss.

After a while, he lifted his head and rested his forehead against hers. 'I'm not going to rush you, Reeza. I couldn't help kissing you.' His lips slid slowly across her cheek and he feathered kisses at the side of her mouth. 'I'll be honest. I haven't felt like this before.'

Reeza lowered her hands and stepped back as her nerves jolted in response to his kiss. 'You're not rushing me, Zac.' She lifted her head and held his gaze. 'I feel the same way.'

'Shall we go to our room?' He pulled her close as his head lowered to hers again.

'I think that would be a very good idea,' Reeza said, her voice husky.

Chapter 11

'I don't care if he's the king of England, I don't like the man.' Dad sat at the kitchen table and glowered at her over the bacon and eggs that Mum had put in front of him. 'He's not our type.'

Reeza's temper grew as she stood in the kitchen at six o'clock on a Thursday three weeks later.

'And,' Dad ignored her question and picked up his fork, jabbing it in the air at her. 'Who does he think he is, keeping you away from home every weekend? From bloody Thursday night? It's not even the weekend. You're not going to stay in the city this weekend. I want you to come home, you're needed here.'

'No,' Reeza said.

Mum shook her head at her

behind Dad's back, but Reeza had had enough.

'Dad. I am twenty-nine years old, I have a career, I earn my own keep, and *you* have no say in what I do on my weekends, or who I see. I'll be home on Sunday afternoon. Zac said he will drive me home.'

'Like I said before, he's not our type.'

And just what is our type, Dad? Someone who goes to the pub, and drinks too much and then has a bet on the horses?'

'No, someone who works a real job, someone who doesn't make money out of other people.'

'So you think that's what I do?'

Yes,' he said tersely. 'A bloody economics degree. I thought it was ridiculous when you enrolled, but I let you do it.'

'You let me do it? I paid my own way, and I have a huge bloody HECS debt, *and* I worked on the farm the whole four years I was studying. What more do you want from me?'

'I want you to give up working in the city, hanging about with ponces that aren't our type, and come home and work in the orchard.'

Reeza picked up the overnight bag she'd packed for the weekend; she was staying at Zac's place in the city tonight, and taking him to her favourite Thai restaurant in Surry Hills for dinner after work.

Her voice was hard and cold. 'I'll see you on Sunday afternoon, and I'd appreciate it if you could be civil to Zac when he brings me home. His mother has invited me to their house and I'm looking forward to meeting her.'

Her father always had to have the last word. 'Christ, and he's a Mummy's boy to boot. How old is he? Still lives with his mother? Jeez, now I've heard it all.'

'No, he hasn't—' Reeza cut her words off. There was no point arguing or explaining herself to Dad. She leaned over and kissed her mother on the cheek. 'I'll see you on Sunday, Mum. Don't work too hard on the weekend, will you? Ted said he'd drive me to the train station this morning. I'll take my stuff out to the garage.'

'He should make you bloody walk,' her father muttered as he shovelled bacon into his mouth.

Reeza rolled her eyes and headed outside. It really was past time she looked at renting a place in the city.

***

Late that afternoon Zac was about to leave his office and meet Reeza in the foyer when the CEO stepped through the door. 'Montgomery, I want you to clear your calendar for the day tomorrow. We've got a serious problem, and we need to spend all day going through transactions and interviewing staff.'

'What sort of problem?'

Gregor Drummond, the CEO waved a dismissive hand. 'I'll fill you in tomorrow. Just clear your calendar. And be here early. Seven a.m. start.'

Zac nodded at Drummond's back as he left the room. The atmosphere in the bank had changed since Drummond had taken over, and Zac was considering his options. The more he had to do with the new CEO, the more he was considering moving on. It was time for a change. He had been planning to take Reeza out for an early breakfast on the harbour and drive her to the office in the morning, but those plans were cactus now.

Zac was preoccupied as he headed down in the elevator. Being surrounded by suits and serious faces depressed him. As he stepped out into the foyer, he looked over towards the bank of elevators that went down to the basement carpark.

His heart lifted as his gaze settled on Reeza. She was sitting on the seat where he'd told her to wait. She'd changed from her dark business suit and her bright pink dress cheered him.

She stood as he walked over

and his heartbeat crept up. He'd worked with Reeza for almost two years, and he'd always found her to be sweet, but after spending the past three weekends with her, he found it hard to stop thinking about her day and night. He'd tried to stay away from the trading floor, but every opportunity that came up, he was out there, mooning around like an adolescent, and not a thirty-seven-year old man. Today he'd made a conscious effort not to go to her floor and then she'd been in his head all day because he'd missed seeing her. Three nights this week, he'd called her when she'd been on the train home to Brentwood, and they'd talked for an hour.

Not about work, or their day, but about all sorts of other things. It had only been three weeks since he'd driven past her that rainy night but he knew her well. The first night they'd spent together—in one room—at the Country Pines Resort, there had been little talking done. Zac had done a double take when he'd seen the charge on his credit card, but spending that night with Reeza had been worth every cent.

The last two weekends she'd stayed in Sydney in his apartment.

He hoped that Reeza was going to be a permanent part of his future. The love word hadn't been mentioned, but he knew he'd fallen head over heels.

He'd made a call today about a night at the Hydro Majestic in the Blue Mountains, and he was going to ask her tonight to come away with him next weekend.

'Hello, Mr Montgomery,' she

said softly as he reached her.

'Good afternoon, Ms Anderson. You are looking very lovely.'

'Thank you, I went shopping in my lunch hour.'

'Don't tell me you wore colour on the trading floor? That would have stirred the old codgers up.'

'Ssh. Someone will hear you,' she said looking around.

'There's no one here. But it wouldn't hurt to stir them up a bit.'

'You don't enjoy working here very much, do you?' she said as they stepped into the empty elevator.

'You're getting to know me well. I'm a bit over the place at the moment. I'm thinking about moving on.'

'Not too far away, I hope?' Disappointment flooded through Reeza as she looked up at him.

Zac put his hands on her shoulders and lowered his lips to hers. The elevator dinged as they reached the basement and he stepped away. 'Don't you worry about that. I won't be going far. And to be honest, it'll make things easier if we don't work at the same place. Come on, let's go. This isn't the right place for this conversation.'

Half an hour later they were sitting at a bench in the Thai restaurant overlooking Oxford Street, waiting for their meals.

'Are you still thinking of buying a property out Brentwood way?' Reeza asked.

Zac linked his fingers with hers as they looked out over the busy street. 'To be honest, I'm not sure now. I think wanting to move out of the city was a bit of a kneejerk reaction to being unsettled at the bank. So maybe not.'

'That's good, because I've decided to move into town. I had another argument with Dad this morning, and I figured it's time to leave home. I think I've got enough saved for a deposit on an apartment.' She looked at him and smiled; Zac's head was close to hers. 'There's a lot of attraction to being in the city all of a sudden.'

'I'm pleased to hear that.'

They moved apart as the waitress stood behind them and reached over with two steaming bowls of laksa.

As they waited for their meals to cool, Reeza looked at Zac curiously. 'No specifics, but why are you unhappy working at the bank? I've always had the impression you loved the place and were pretty much wedded to your job.' He hesitated and she put up her hand. 'No, that was out of line. You're my boss, and I have no right to ask you that.'

Zac reached over and took her hand. 'You know I'd like to be more than a boss to you, Reeza, so you have a right to know what makes me happy. We've come a long way from a working relationship in three weeks.' He let out a long sigh, and she frowned. 'The management ethos has changed a lot over the past year. It probably hasn't filtered down to the trading floor, but the direction of the new strategic plan doesn't sit comfortably with me. I guess dreaming about buying a farm and leaving the bank was an escape. It might sound like bragging, but I've made an obscene amount of money in the fifteen years I've worked there. I could afford to retire now, but really, what would I do? How would I fill my days?'

Reeza nodded. 'I know what you mean. You dream of what you think you want out of a career, and then you find that it's other things in life that you really want, but if you want to get those things, you have to keep up with the career to earn enough money to get what you want out of life.'

'So you're not happy at the bank either, by the sound of that.'

'I am, but like you, there has been a change in the atmosphere. I hope it'll go back to what it used to be eventually. Bosses come and go, management practice changes. I love the work I do, and it might sound as though I'm bragging too, but I'm very good at it. I've made a lot of money for the bank in the last six months. It's good to be appreciated and recognised; it's not something that happens anywhere else in my life. But it's a job where I will achieve my dream. I want to make enough money to get what I want out of life.'

'And your goal is to get your dream apartment like you told me that night at the Country Pines.'

Reeza smiled. 'I think my dream is more about having my own space than anything luxurious. Although luxury would be nice. What about you, Zac? If you could do exactly what you wanted, would you really go cruising?'

He shook his head as she looked across at him. His eyes were dancing and a surge of attraction hit her squarely in her lower belly. As it had regularly over the last three weeks. 'Do you think that's a foolish dream?'

'No dreams are foolish. They are a part of us.' She couldn't help reaching out and touching his arm. Skin to skin contact eased that desire a little bit. At least it did until Zac ran his fingers up and down the inside of her wrist, and the desire surged back. Getting to know him as a person over the past few weeks, rather than as the aloof boss, had stirred something deep in her. 'So tell me more about your dream.'

'I love being on the water. I'd love to be more adventurous. I'd like to challenge myself. Go places where there is little in the way of civilisation. The West coast. The Kimberleys.'

'It's a big dream. And an adventure to boot.'

'What about you? Are you a boat person?' he asked as he stopped stroking her arm and picked up his spoon. 'Could I tempt you to come with me?'

'Really?' Reeza picked up her spoon. 'Now you have to promise not to laugh.'

'Okay.'

'Growing up on the orchard meant very few trips into town, and even fewer holidays when I was growing up. The sum total of my boating experience is the small punt that we had down on our back dam when we were kids.'

'Sounds like I will have to take you out on the harbour.'

'You have a boat already?'

'Just a small one, but it's fed my dream for the past ten years.'

'Sounds like it might be the time to follow that dream.'

'Could be,' he said.

Chapter 12

Zac found it hard to leave Tess at five a.m. the next morning. He'd set the alarm on low volume, but she'd still woken up when he did.

'Stay there,' he said as she went to climb out of his bed. 'You've got another couple of hours before you have to get up.'

'No, I'll have a cuppa with you.' She swung her long legs over the side of the bed and reached for the T-shirt that had barely covered her thighs last night.

Zac groaned and pulled her close. 'Do you know how hard it is not to climb back into bed with you? The last thing I want to do is go to the office and have a day closeted with Bulldog.'

'Bulldog? That's what you call the CEO?'

Zac nodded and looked a bit embarrassed. 'That was very unprofessional. Forget I said that.'

'Forgotten already.' Reeza nodded and then reached up to kiss him. 'We have all weekend ahead of us.'

'I wasn't disappointed when Mum decided to go to Newcastle to the art gallery. She'll be back for lunch tomorrow.'

'I'm looking forward to meeting her.' She stepped back and let him go. 'Now go and have a shower and I'll put the coffee on.'

'Are you right to get to George Street from here? Grab a cab.'

'No, that's a waste of money. The bus will get me there.'

'Okay, if you're happy with that.' Zac shrugged and looked after Reeza as she went into the kitchen. He had never had to take public transport. His respect for her grew each day. He'd grown up in an affluent family, and they had had a good income. When his father had walked out on them when Zac was ten, his mother had a high income and there'd been no hardship. It had been a natural progression for him to follow that path, but more and more lately, he'd been dissatisfied with his life.

Reeza was very different to him, extremely conscious of what she spent, and she'd told him how she had almost paid her HECS debt off, and had saved enough for a deposit on an apartment. She'd only been at the bank for two years and he was amazed by how much she'd managed to save in such a short time. He wondered if she knew how much of a deposit she'd need in the city. Sometimes her naivete surprised him, but it was refreshing, and one of the things he was beginning to love about her.

Zac had fallen, and fallen hard. Even though it had been less than a month, he was going to ask her to move in with him when they went to the Blue Mountains. It could be a trial run, and it would save her that long commute in and out of town each day. And she wouldn't have to worry about looking for an apartment. He imagined she wouldn't be able to afford anything within a twenty kilometre—or more—radius of the inner city.

Fifteen minutes later, Zac had showered, shaved and dressed in one of the corporate suits he was beginning to hate.

'What's that sad face all

about?' Reeza asked as she passed him a coffee. Her hair was tousled, and her cheeks flushed pink, and Zac thought he'd never seen a more beautiful sight.

'I'd much rather be doing something with you than spending the day in a monkey suit in Gregor Drummond's office.'

'I wondered why you had to go in so early.' She looked at him curiously. 'What's happening?'

Zac shook his head. 'Who knows. He's got a bee in his bonnet about something. I'm going in early at his direction, but I'm not working back. It's Friday night and we're going somewhere special for dinner.'

'Are we?' A sexy smile tilted her lips. 'I was thinking we could stay in and have an early night before your mother comes home tomorrow.' Her dark brown eyes were full of mischief. 'You'll be tired after all your meetings, and we'll probably need a big sleep-in in the morning too. Did I tell you how comfortable your bed is?'

'Is that the only attraction here, witch? My soft bed?' Zac pulled her close and kissed her. 'You are a temptress, madame, but I think that's an excellent idea. I'll meet you in the basement at five-fifteen and we'll pick up something for dinner on the way back here.'

'I'll look forward to it.' Her breasts were soft against his chest as she pressed closer to him and looped her arms around his neck. 'You have a good day, and I'll see you this afternoon.' She stood on her toes and her lips were warm against his.

'Okay. Time to go.' Finally he

pulled away, and couldn't help himself. He would ask her tonight, not next weekend. 'I have something to ask you at dinner.'

'What?' Her smile was cheeky.

'You'll have to wait.'

'Oh, that's mean. Now I'll wonder what it is all day. Will I like it?'

'I hope so.' Zac ran his finger down Reeza's nose to her lips. 'Have a good day.' He whistled happily as he pulled the door shut behind him and headed to the garage beside the house. It was going to be an excellent weekend.

***

Reeza's day went downhill from the minute she crossed the road outside Zac's mother's house and saw the bus she'd hoped to catch heading away from her through the traffic lights. She glanced at her watch; it was half an hour until the next bus was due, and it would be after nine before she reached the bank. Despite being two floors above her, she knew the CEO kept an eagle eye on each level and the arrival and departure times of each employee. Sitting opposite Brad Drummond—who took advantage of being the boss's son and had extra-long lunch breaks—Reeza had no doubt that if she was late, her lateness would be noted and passed onto his father. She hated the lack of trust in the organisation; they were responsible adults, and knew what was required without being checked on as though they were still at school. The atmosphere had become toxic since Drummond had taken over, but still she had been surprised to hear Zac criticise him.

The new culture at the office was the main reason that she and Zac were keeping their—their what?—under wraps.

Relationship? Romance? Fling? Anyway, whatever it was, they were keeping it private. Even though they had agreed to keep things the same at work, Zac hadn't seemed worried about taking her out in the city. The word would filter back one day, and she knew it wouldn't go down well with the CEO.

Not that there was a policy about it, but there were strict expectations about confidentiality. After Drummond had taken over as CEO, one of the women on her floor had transferred to another bank, because both she and her husband worked for the bank. Crazy, Reeza had thought. That would be more of a conflict of interest.

She knew that she was more uncomfortable than Zac was, but he'd agreed to keep things at a low profile.

It was all right for him; he'd had the promotions and had reached a high level in the bank, even though he did seem discontented there. Reeza didn't want to put her position in jeopardy at the beginning of her career, and just when her work was getting noticed.

She stepped to the edge of the footpath and hailed the vacant taxi cruising down Peronne Avenue. There'd been a pile of incoming transactions on her desk when she'd left last night, and it would be good to get in early and get them cleared.

The traffic was heavy as they crossed the Spit Bridge, but it lightened as they approached the city.

To Reeza's surprise Brad Drummond was sitting at her desk when she walked onto the trading floor twenty minutes before nine. He was the only one in the room and was looking through the papers in her in-tray.

'What are you doing, Brad?' Reeza asked as she hurried across to her desk. It was an unwritten law on the floor that a banker's desk was private.

He jumped and when he turned around his eyes were narrowed. 'Morning, Theresa.'

'What are you looking for?' she persisted.

'I was after a red pen.'

'I don't have one.'

He kept sitting there looking up at her, a smug look on his face. 'You're early. Stayed in town, did you?'

'Early enough to catch you going through my files. Red pen, be buggered,' she said. Reeza was angry. 'I don't believe a word you're saying. Do it again and I'll report you, Brad.'

He rolled her chair back and laughed. 'Will you just? And who are you going to report me to? Zaccy boy?'

'What?' Her breath caught as unease grabbed her. She could feel the heat rising up her neck as he stood and looked down at her. He was an unattractive man, and he took no pride in cleanliness; his clothes smelled stale and there was a definite whiff of body odour emanating from him.

'You and Zachary were very cosy together at *Lom Sam* last night. Don't you worry, sweetheart, sleeping with Zac's not going to get you a promotion. Or out of trouble.' He put a hand to his mouth and chuckled. 'Oops, not yet. You're a woman, and my father won't have a female trader in his bank.'

Reeza was lost for words as a myriad of emotions gripped her. She knew that Brad was just mouthing off. Drummond was savvy enough to know that a rumour like that would put his position as CEO at risk.

'You talk garbage, Bradley. It's not *his* bank and I don't imagine the board would be impressed to hear a sexist statement like that. And whatever I do in my own time is my business and none of yours.'

Her voice was calm and controlled as she pushed past him. She froze when Brad grabbed her arm. 'You think you're pretty fucking special, don't you?' Reeza stared at him, horrified as spit flew from his mouth and just missed her face. 'You can be as cocky as you like now, Theresa, but let's see what the day brings.'

She sat at her desk ignoring him but her hands shook as she put her handbag in the drawer. As he went back to his own desk, Brad laughed and a shiver ran down her back. Turning her computer on, she logged in and reached for the transactions awaiting her attention. With a frown, she flicked through them; she thought there'd been more than that. Maybe she'd been wrong, but she wondered what Brad had been doing with them.

Three hours later Reeza finally looked up as Brad stood and disappeared for his usual lunch break. She had not spoken to him, or looked at him since she'd started work. Leaning back, she stretched her arms and looked around. The floor was quiet today; there was a strange atmosphere in the office.

She opened the desk drawer and took her purse from her handbag, and made her way to the elevator. Zac was occasionally down near the sandwich shop on the floor below reception when she went down at lunchtime, but she didn't hold out much hope today; he'd said it was an all-day meeting. Knowing Drummond, they'd have a fully catered lunch.

Reeza purchased an egg salad roll and a takeaway coffee and

headed back to the floor. She'd stay close to her desk; she didn't want Brad going through her files again. From today, she'd be more careful of what she left in her tray overnight. For a moment, she wondered about raising it with Zac, and then realised that was the very thing she didn't want to do. She wasn't going to take advantage of their relationship.

Two of the guys from her floor were in the small kitchen that doubled as a lunchroom. Reeza sat at the table with them, but apart from a brief nod her way as they each looked up from their phones, there was no conversation, which was unusual.

Worry nagged at her; she wondered if Brad had been mouthing off about seeing her out with Zac last night. With a sigh, she pushed away her bread roll, and reached for her coffee. Her appetite had gone.

Finally, Steven, the guy opposite her, looked up from his phone and spoke quietly. 'I noticed you've had your head down all morning, Theresa. Just a heads up, you're likely to be called into the boss's office after lunch. We've both been grilled this morning and it wasn't pleasant.'

Paul looked up and nodded. 'No, it wasn't.'

'Grilled about what? And whose office? Zac Montgomery's?'

Paul pulled a face. 'No, the big boss, Drummond. It was so unpleasant I wished I'd asked for a support person, or the union guy to come in with me.'

'What's it all about?' she asked with a frown.

Paul and Steven exchanged a glance. 'Better off to let you go in cold,' Steven said. 'Just be careful what you say though. Drummond won't be left looking bad. There's been a dud transaction, and he won't take the fall for it. Just answer what he asks and don't be tempted to say anything else.'

'About anybody,' Paul added.

'No one,' Steven said with a nod.

Reeza knew exactly who they were talking about.

Brad Drummond.

'Thanks, guys.' She stood and put the last half of her lunch in the bin. 'I'll get back to work. Hopefully I won't get called in.'

'Hope you don't,' Steven said. 'I'm pleased it's the weekend. It's been a shit of a day.'

Reeza went back to her desk,

and even though she had plenty of work to keep her occupied, the afternoon dragged. Every time the door opened, she expected to be called in and her stomach was tight with tension.

The worst of it was that she knew if she got called in, that Zac would be in there too, and she would have to be very careful with her reactions, and her responses.

Brad didn't come back from lunch, and that worried her too. She'd stood up to him, and she'd seen the nastiness in his expression. She didn't trust him. With a sigh she tried to focus on her work. The next time she looked at the clock on her computer, it was five minutes before five, and relief flooded through her. She'd obviously missed out on a grilling and could start to look forward to the weekend.

Probably because she was too junior to have any initiatives that could be questioned. Her level of work was a bit like a glorified clerk, although she had spotted some opportunities that had been acted upon a couple of months ago.

As the bell went, indicating local trading was over, Reeza took her handbag from the drawer and stood. As she shut down the computer, the door opened and Drummond's executive assistant came in and walked over to her.

'Mr Drummond would like to see you, Ms Anderson.'

She glanced up at the clock on the wall. 'Now?' She was supposed to be meeting Zac in fifteen minutes in the basement car park.

He nodded. 'Yes, now.'

She went to put her bag away,

but he shook his head. 'Bring your bag with you. You'll be leaving after the meeting. Do you have any other personal effects in the office?'

Reeza frowned, not understanding what he meant. 'Personal effects?'

'Anything that belongs to you.'

'No, I don't.'

'Very well. Come with me, please.'

The air in the corridor was cold and smelled sterile. Reeza found it difficult to walk after him to the elevator. Her knees were shaking, and her legs were like jelly, and her heels clicked loudly on the tiled floor as she followed him into the elevator. The silence was fraught with tension, and Reeza's stomach clenched.

'I need to use the bathroom

before I see Mr Drummond please,' she said politely.

'Very well, but I'll take your handbag.' The assistant escorted her to the entrance to the ladies' room and then held his hand out for her bag.

'I beg your pardon? Why do you have to hold my bag?' She stared at him, confused by his instruction.

'For security.'

'Why?'

He looked at her as though she was being difficult. 'So you can't remove anything from your bag.'

Reeza held her tongue and passed her bag over and went into the ladies. On the way to the cubicle, she caught sight of herself in the mirror.

Gone was the happy, glowing face that had looked back at her from the ensuite mirror in Zac's bedroom this morning. In its place was a pale wide-eyed face that showed her lack of confidence; a dreadful feeling of foreboding gripped her. Brad's words kept going around in her head. *You can be as cocky as you like now, Theresa, but let's see what the day brings.* The fact that he hadn't come back to the floor also worried her. It had been a very strange day.

Reeza came out of the toilet cubicle, washed her face and hands, and then pinched her cheeks; she looked slightly better as she went back into the corridor.

'This way, please, Ms Anderson.'

Reeza swallowed as she followed him into the inner sanctum where she had never been before.

Chapter 13

Zac sat straight and held his breath as the door opened. Reeza stepped in and looked first at Drummond and then at him. It was impossible to read her expression.

It was almost impossible to hide his anger and disgust. She had played him for the utter fool he was. As Drummond had laid out each piece of evidence against Reeza, Zac had examined them with intense focus. To the best of his knowledge, the CEO didn't know that they'd been seeing each other.

Christ, he'd been going to ask her to move in with him. And she was going to meet his mother tomorrow.

An absolute fool. Theresa Anderson had played him to

perfection. He lifted his head and stared at her when she sat down. They were sitting informally on three soft chairs around a low table.

Her face was pale and her green eyes shimmered. Reeza knew she'd been caught out. She widened her eyes and raised her eyebrows as she lifted her eyes to meet his.

Zac looked away, and next time he looked at her, her face was white.

Guilty as sin. Had she known he was going to Brentwood that night and timed her walk in the rain so he'd pick her up? Or was that stretching it? The rest of the evidence was there and it made him sick to the stomach. All the guff about saving for an apartment. Christ, she had more in her investment portfolio than he did.

'Thank you for meeting with us, Ms Anderson,' Drummond said evenly.

Zac looked at her again, and she inclined her head. It was hard to believe this was the pink-faced woman who had been in his bed last night. If he'd been asked to describe a guilty person, he could describe Reeza's face.

'I don't understand what this is about,' she replied. 'Or why you need to talk to me.' Her voice was quiet, but still familiar enough to wrench Zac's heart.

'There has been a serious breach in the security of our foreign transactions and it has cost the bank a considerable amount of money. There have been breakdowns in internal controls.

We have some questions for you. I'll hand over to Mr Montgomery as your direct supervisor.'

'I hope you will answer my question honestly, and with as much information as you can, Ms Anderson. Any information that you withhold will go against you.' Zac kept his voice formal.

Her bottom lip trembled, and all he could think about was how soft her lips had felt beneath his. He reached for the folder on the table in front of them. The knowledge that he had been duped—both personally and professionally—came rushing back, and his tone was curt and hard when he spoke.

'On Friday the fifteenth of last month, you completed a transaction in Swiss dollars that breached bank protocol. Can you please explain the nature of that transaction to us?'

Her voice was surprisingly even as she lifted her eyes to hold his. '*Mr* Montgomery, since the fifteenth of last month I would have handled hundreds of transactions and many in Swiss dollars, none of which have breached protocol. If you would like me to explain a particular one, you will have to be more specific.'

Zac removed the printout of the transaction that Reeza had pocketed a neat seven hundred thousand dollars from, and handed it to her. She didn't need to know yet, that the deposit into her account was now on record. Her fingers brushed his as she took the paper, and he cursed himself for being every kind of fool under the sun as the nerves in his arm kicked from her brief touch.

He sat back and folded his arms as he watched her read it. Slowly the little remaining colour leached from her lips.

'This is not my work.'

'I beg to differ,' he said. 'The keystrokes have been audited as being directly from both your log in and from the computer in your office.' He glanced down at the copy of the transaction that he had retained. 'At five twenty-seven on the fifteenth of March.'

Her face cleared and he didn't like the smile that crossed her face.

'You do realise, Ms Anderson, that this will result in the termination of your employment,' Drummond's voice filled the silence.

'I don't think it will, Mr

Drummond.' Her voice was clear and true, and Zac shook his head. 'I can prove it wasn't me.'

Reeza went to speak, and then she looked at Zac and closed her mouth. Confusion crossed her face, and she dropped her gaze to her hands as though she was considering something. She sat like that for a full five minutes until the CEO cleared his throat. When she lifted her head, her eyes were sad, and Zac found it hard to stay strong.

'If you check with security records, you will see that I have never stayed past five o'clock. Her voice strengthened. 'The fact that I couldn't stay back had bothered me, but on this occasion it appears that I will be vindicated because of that stupid rule.'

The CEO leaned forward. 'Mr

Montgomery?'

Zac pulled out the next piece of paper that recorded her departure from the trading floor at five forty on that afternoon. Until he'd seen that security record, he'd doubted her guilt, but when he'd examined the data for the third time, and listened to the evidence of the other traders on the floor, he knew he'd been trying to find excuses because he didn't want to believe Reeza was guilty.

Theresa Anderson was not the woman he had thought she was. The woman he had kidded himself into believing he had fallen in love with.

'Ms Anderson, there is a detective in the foyer waiting to take you to the police station to be charged. There is a security guard outside who will take you down to meet him.'

Even knowing her guilt, when Reeza began to stand and then fell back into the chair, all Zac wanted to do was hold her and protect her.

Not caring what Drummond thought, Zac leaned forward and put his head in his hands as Reeza sobbed.

'I didn't do anything wrong.'

Chapter 14
Pentecost Island

'Theresa.' When Zac's deep voice came from the forest behind her, Tess put her hand to her throat. Her legs began to shake uncontrollably and she grabbed for the tree that was beside her.

'What the hell are you doing here?' Her voice shook so much she wasn't sure if her words were clear enough to be understood. She let go of the tree and wrapped her arms across her chest. Despite the hot humid night, her blood was chilled, and goose bumps rose on her skin as she shivered.

'I need you to keep a secret.' Zac walked towards her and she took a step back.

'What? Are you for real? What

the bloody hell are you doing here? Can't you leave me alone. You've already ruined my life. Why are you hounding me? How much more damage can you do? Just go away!'

'I need to talk to you, Reeza. I have to talk to you.'

She twisted around so quickly she saw stars. 'Don't you dare call me that. My name is Tess.'

His voice was quiet. 'It suits you. So does the hair.' Zac leaned forward, so close she could feel his breath on her skin. For one awful moment she thought he was going to touch her. The worst thing was, for all the hatred that had consumed her over the past two years, Tess knew Zac's touch would bring her undone. 'And the blue eyes,' he said. 'If I hadn't tracked you down and verified it was you, I would never have recognised you.'

'Why? What have you tracked me down for? Are you going to call the police? The media? I can just see the headline. Woman on the run found in tropical paradise.'

'No, listen to me.'

'No, you listen to me. Leave me alone! Just leave me in peace to get on with my life. Haven't you done enough damage already?'

'I need to talk you to you, Ree—'

'Why?' Her voice shook as the futility of it all overwhelmed her.

The waste.

Her university study.

The hard work she'd done for two years.

Reinventing herself, finding safety on the island, a new career and now having Zac turn up with no warning and—

'Wait a minute,' she said. 'How did you get here? Did you book in under a false name? And what do you mean, verified it was me?'

As she stood there staring at him, voices reached them as someone walked from the bar through the glade.

'Quickly. Please listen to me. I'm known as Monty these days. Rafe knows me and he knows why I'm here. You can let people know we knew each other in the past but don't mention the bank. Please . . . Tess . . please. Trust me. I'll explain everything later.'

Trust him!

Not a snowball's chance in hell of that. Reeza trusted no one these days. As she stared at Zac wondering what the hell he was up to, and what she should do, Pippa and Rafe walked into the glade.

'There you are, Tess. We were coming to see what was holding you up. The party's in full swing.'

'I was running the weekly backup, and then I went to get changed. And then'—she flicked a glance to Zac—'then on the way here I bumped into . . . Monty.'

The relief on his face was clear and Zac smiled at Tess before he turned to Rafe. 'I was walking over from the pool area, and I literally bumped into Tess. Neither of us could believe it.'

Pippa turned to Rafe. 'Are you going to introduce us?'

'Sorry, love, I forgot you hadn't met Monty. Monty, this is my wife, Phillipa, known to all as Pippa. Pippa knows about you, and what a great job you'll do.'

Tess looked from one to the other wondering what job Zac—

Monty—was going to do on the island. As far as she knew it wasn't the place for an investment banker. He wasn't a guest; she racked her brains as she ran the guest list through her head. There had been no Monty anything on it.

As Zac held his hand out and shook Pippa's hand, Tess took the opportunity to study him. He'd changed in the past two years, as she had. His hair was longer and curled onto his neck, his skin held a deeper tan, but most of all—and strangely—he'd grown. He had obviously been working out, because his muscles were much more defined and his shoulders seemed broader. When he had been her boss, he had been good looking but in an urbane sort of way. Back then he had been fit— lithe and taut—now he was *big*, and had a sort of roughness that had been polished out of him before.

'Good to meet, you, Pippa. I've heard a lot about you from Rafe.'

'Have you?' Pippa said. 'Welcome aboard. It's good to have you here. I'm sorry I wasn't at your interview. It was a manic day.'

Tess's head turned from left to right as she followed the conversation. An interview? Even though she hadn't met him, Pippa obviously knew why he was here.

Zac had a job here? That was the last thing that Tess would have guessed in a million years.

'So, let's head back to the party,' Pippa said with a smile. 'A great opportunity for you to meet the rest of the staff. I'll leave Tess to introduce you around.'

Great, she thought. Just great. She could barely function now that Zac had stunned her with his arrival on the island. She knew nothing about him now, or why he was here, looking so buff and tanned, and she was going to introduce him to everyone?

Fear ate away at her. She didn't want to leave here, but if he was going to open his mouth and say who she was, she would be gone tomorrow.

Maybe she could develop a migraine in the next two minutes. Before she could open her mouth, Pippa and Rafe headed back to the bar, and Zac took her hand and tucked it into the crook of his arm.

He leaned down and whispered. 'I'll explain everything later.'

Tess jerked her arm away. 'Too

bloody right you will. And then you'll leave.'

Chapter 15
Sydney -Two years earlier

Reeza had no memory of riding down to the foyer in the elevator with the security guard accompanying her. She blinked as he led her out into the foyer. She wasn't sure where they were supposed to be going.

'Will you be all right, Ms Anderson?' Ken, the security guy she'd greeted every morning for two years looked at her with concern. He knew she wasn't a thief and a criminal. Why did he have to take her to a detective, and then what was going to happen? Surely no one really believed she was a criminal.

'This way.' As he touched her elbow gently and steered her to the right, his phone rang. 'Excuse me, a moment. He turned away from her; he obviously trusted her. Reeza blinked, wondering if she was asleep and in the middle of a bad dream.

'Yes, sir. No problem. Yes, I will.'

As he disconnected there was a bright flash. Reeza turned wide-eyed, and another flash went off.

'That's her,' a man in a suit stood beside the photographer. 'Miss Anderson,' he called out as he came closer.

Ken grabbed her arm. 'Come into my room, love, and I'll get rid of the newspaper vultures.'

Reeza shook her head. 'Why are they here? Who called them?'

'I don't know.' He opened the door to his small room off the foyer and when Reeza was inside, he closed it. 'I'll be back in a minute.'

There was a plastic chair next

to the desk and she sat on it and put her bag on the floor. Shaking her head, she rubbed her hand over her eyes, trying to make sense of what had happened. The CEO had accused her of fraud, and she'd had no chance to defend herself. As for Zac, his behaviour made her feel sick to the stomach.

After a few minutes the door opened. 'The coast's clear. I've put the skids under them. You can go.'

'Go where? To the police station?'

'Oh, sorry, Ms Anderson. Those bloody journalists distracted me. Mr Drummond rang down. I'm to allow you to leave. The charges have been dropped.'

'So I still have a job?'

He stared at her for a moment and then shook his head. 'I'm sorry. No. I'm really sorry, love.

I'm sure you've noticed things aren't good here. This isn't the first time I've had to tell a staff member this. If you enter the building the police will be called.'

Reeza nodded. 'Thank you for being kind to me. I'll go now. I'll leave. I'll . . .um. . . guess I'll go home.'

By home, she meant home to Brentwood. She couldn't face Zac at the moment, not after he'd sat there and let her face those ridiculous accusations. She'd wait until he rang—if he rang—and see what he had to say. As far as spending this weekend with him, all desire to do that had gone.

In fact, Reeza was finding it hard to think. 'Thank you, Ken.' She smiled at him and was surprised to see that everything was hazy, through a blur of tears.

She had lost her job.

Hitching her handbag over her shoulder, she walked out the main bank doors for the last time. It was a crisp autumn evening. The muted roar of traffic from the Cahill Expressway filled the air, punctuated by blaring horns and the roar of a bus as it accelerated past the building. As she tried to focus on which way to go, a movement and another flash on the footpath caught her attention.

'Theresa.' She turned slowly and stared at the man in the crumpled grey suit. 'A word, love?'

She frowned. 'A word?'

'Tell us what happened in there. Have you been charged? What did you do? What have you done with the money? Almost a million, they said.'

Horror filled her as she realised

it was the journalist again. As she stared at him, her mouth open and tears rolling down her cheeks, a man with a large camera on his shoulder stepped between them. She turned and ran, ran as fast as she could, weaving through back streets, up and down steep streets until she had no idea where she was. Finally all was quiet, and she stopped to catch her breath and looked around. An old hotel sat on the corner opposite her and when she turned and saw the pylons of the Harbour Bridge above her, Reeza realised she had come under the Expressway and was on the other side of The Rocks.

A long way from any train station, but she'd probably missed the last train south anyway. As she contemplated what to do—she could always go back to Zac's house—her phone buzzed in her handbag.

She reached in and pulled it out and the screen lit up; it was Mum.

'Mum?' she said quietly.

'No, it's not your mother. She's hysterical in the kitchen,' Dad roared. 'What the bloody hell is going on, Theresa? What have you done?'

'Done? I've done nothing. Why, what's wrong with Mum?'

'There's a bloody helicopter in the paddock. Journalists crawling all over the place, waiting for you to get home, and you're plastered all over the six o'clock TV news. What the fuck have you done, girl?'

Reeza gasped. In all of her twenty-nine years, she had never once heard Dad use the F word. 'I haven't done anything wrong.'

'They said you were at the police station, being charged. Why would they say that?' His voice had quietened a fraction.

'Because they're lying. It was all a mistake. I'm trying to find a way home.'

'Don't you dare come home. I thought you were going to the precious boyfriend's mother's place for the weekend. Or are the media there too?'

Reeza sighed. 'I don't know.'

'Where are you?'

'I'm lost.'

Finally a bit of concern in Dad's voice. 'Are you safe where you are?'

'I think so.'

'Good. I'll put your mother on.'

Reeza waited for a full minute before her mother took the phone.

'Theresa, Dad said you're lost.

Where are you?'

'In the city. Dad said you were hysterical, There's no need to be, Mum.'

'I wasn't bloody hysterical. I was yelling at him, because he got his shotgun out and he was going to fire it over the heads of the journalists. I was simply yelling at him to stop.'

'Oh, God. And did he?' Reeza put her hand to her head.

'Yes, he did. But they're all camped out there waiting for you to come home. Bloody dozens of them. Cameras and all. We told them you weren't coming home. Where's Zac, Theresa? And how did you get lost?'

'Long story, Mum.' Reeza bit her lip as she decided what to do. It was hard to think straight. 'Can you do me a really, really big favour?'

'What do you want me to do?'

'Can you go into my room and pack me a bag with some clean undies, and my shorts and T-shirts, dresses, and my toiletries and meet me in town.'

'What? Tonight?'

'No tomorrow, will do.'

'All right. I'll get one of the boys to drive me in.' Mum lowered her voice. 'What's Zac's mother's address.'

'I won't be there. I'll meet you at Central Station.'

'Why?'

'I'm going to go away for a while.' Reeza's lip quivered. 'I lost my job today, Mum. They sacked me and I did nothing wrong.'

'Oh, Theresa. I'm sorry, love. But you don't have to go away. You can come home and work in the orchard.'

'No.' Reeza stared up at the bridge. The coloured lights were on, and the flash of headlights and taillights illuminated the pylons in a myriad of blues and reds and whites as commuters made their way home. 'I'm leaving. I'll see you tomorrow. I'll wait in the coffee shop in Eddy Street after nine. The one under the back of the station.'

'All right, if that's what you think is the right thing for you. You always have been the strongest of our three. You take care tonight, and get yourself unlost.'

Reeza chuckled, but her breath caught and it turned into a sob. 'I am "unlost", Mum. I know where I am now, and I've found somewhere to stay tonight.' She stared over as the Vacancy sign lit up outside the Lord Nelson Hotel.

'Goodnight, Mum.'

She opened her phone and pulled the SIM cad out and broke it in half. There was no way the media would track her.

Chapter 16
Pippa - Pentecost Island

I sat beside Rafe on a stool at the bar and reached for my glass. The soda water bubbles tickled my nose as I lifted it to sip slowly. Nat had looked at me curiously when I had asked for soda water in a champagne glass. If Nell said anything about it later, I'd say I'd had enough wine.

I actually hadn't had any. To my horror, I had missed two periods, but I hadn't told a soul. Not even Rafe. And that added to my guilt.

Rafe turned back to face me when Dylan left the bar and got Odessa up for a dance.

'He's a good guy,' Rafe said. 'He was asking about the gardens around the pool, and I told him it was a party and no work talk allowed.'

'He is. He and Odessa are looking very lovey-dovey.'

'I've never seen her so happy, in all the time I've known her. She's really excited about the store opening in Vi's house once the staff move up the hill. Have you seen some of the silver pieces she's made?'

'I have and she's really good.' I reached over and put my hand on my husband's arm. 'And Rafe, I really like her. After a rocky start, she's settled in here well. She came up and had a coffee with me a couple of days ago when she brought some of jewellery up to show me.'

'I'm pleased you've become friends.'

'Speaking of which,'—I moved

closer and lowered my voice—'tell me about this Monty. I thought you said his name was Zac when he was going to be interviewed.'

I'd been watching Monty and Tess since they'd walked to the bar with us. Monty had stopped at a table at the edge of the restaurant away from everyone, but I'd seen Tess shake her head and he'd followed her to a table where Sienna and Danny, and Eliza and Phillipe were sitting. Tess's body language was off, and she was pale.

I knew I was like a mother hen to my friends. Some people saw them as our staff—Eliza, Tam and Nell were part owners of Ma Carmichael's, but I considered all of the staff as friends. I cared about them, and I wanted to make sure they were happy. There'd been some difficult situations since Tam and Nell and I had moved to the island, but everything had settled, the staff all seemed happy, and the building and development were ahead of schedule. We had created a unique establishment here and it was going to be better than we had ever dared dream.

Rafe looked at me, and then turned away.

'Rafe? That's your guilty look. What aren't you telling me?'

He put his arm around my shoulder and chuckled. 'You know me too well, Mrs Rendell.'

'I do. What are you up to?'

'Remember the day Sienna and Danny came back from Esculanta Island and you were going to interview him?'

'Yes, I do, and then there was an emergency up at the building site, and you interviewed him for me and gave him the job.' I narrowed my eyes. 'Zachary Johnson, you said his name was that day. Is Monty a nickname?'

'Sort of.'

'Rafe, what are you up to? You said he was perfect for the job. And I trust you. What's going on?'

'He is perfect, and he's a great guy. Now, Pip, this is for your ears only. He uses Johnson, his mother's name, because he hates people knowing who he is.'

'Who is he? A movie star or something? He could be, he's easy enough on the eye.'

Rafe cleared his throat. 'Um, have you heard me talk about my mate, Zac Montgomery?'

'Ah, yes,' I said slowly, as the light began to dawn. 'Zac Montgomery with the massive boat, you've been friends with for a couple of years. The one I've never met because he's been cruising around the Australian coast.'

'Yes, that's the one.'

'Can't be. Jiminy told me once they call him the bad boy billionaire of Hamo. He doesn't like him.'

'He's just jealous of his boat.'

'He is not!' I burred up. 'Rafe. What's going on? Why do we have a millionaire playboy as our pool lifeguard and why is he here before the pool is finished?'

'Zac is a good man, and has been a good friend to me. He has a problem, and I knew we could help. And it was all in the timing. Don't worry, we're not paying him. He wants to be known as Monty so no one realises he's the guy who owns *Myr*, the big cruiser in the marina over there.'

I slid out from beneath his arm and wagged a finger at him. 'You'll have a problem if you don't tell me what's going on.' I winced as a muscle seemed to pull in my stomach.

'Well, I—' He stopped as I doubled over and put my hand on my stomach. 'What's wrong?' His eyes were wide as he reached for my hand. 'Are you okay?'

The sudden pain had eased, and I shook my head. 'I'm okay, now—' Another sudden pain gripped me and I felt the warm dampness between my thighs. It wasn't the usual monthly pain. This was a lot worse. 'Quick, we need to go back to the house.'

I was embarrassed, but luckily I had on a dark dress, and we managed to leave without drawing any attention to ourselves.

I doubled over again when we reached the stairs at the base of the cliff, and Rafe's eyes were filled with concern as he lifted me into his arms and carried me up the hill to our home.

'Hush, sweetheart, it's okay,' he whispered as I began to cry.

Chapter 17

Zac couldn't keep his eyes off Reeza as she chatted to the others at the table. Once she'd introduced him as Monty, the conversation had been casual, as he'd been welcomed, and then she'd pretty much ignored him.

But he knew those nervous gestures.

Tess, he corrected himself, not Reeza. She looked so different, but still the same. The blonde short hair suited her. It accentuated her high cheekbones and made her eyes look bigger. The one thing he couldn't get used to was the blue eyes. He'd spent a lot of time looking into those pretty green eyes that he knew were now behind coloured lens.

God, what he'd done to her, and what it had done to her life. His stomach churned as he thought about it, and as he wondered what was the best way to get her to listen to him.

Zac had been looking for Reeza for a long time, and he knew now that her family had sent him on a wild goose chase to Western Australia.

Not that he could blame them. They had been protecting her. What the media had done to Theresa Anderson was almost criminal, considering she had been innocent of any wrongdoing.

What had amazed him was how quickly she had managed to disappear into thin air. In a few hours. She'd left her bag at his mother's house—it had been on his boat for the past two years—and as far as he could discover she had never gone home that night.

'Monty? Monty?' The name was said more loudly the second time, and then Zac realised he was being addressed.

'Sorry, Eliza. I was miles away. What did you say?'

'I shouldn't talk about this tonight, but I just wanted to check if you could meet with Pippa and me tomorrow at the pool site. We have a couple of questions about the pool shape from a safety point of view. I wouldn't ask but the form workers had a couple of questions about putting in the day bed platforms on each side. We were lucky Renzo's concreting workers were free and if we sort this tomorrow the concrete will be poured before Christmas.'

'Sure.' Zac was aware of Tess's

close scrutiny. Her eyes had narrowed when Eliza had asked him about the pool. 'Just give me a time and I'll be there.'

'Have you started work already or are you just over for tonight?' Eliza asked.

'I'm going back with Jiminy tonight, but I'll come back over tomorrow. I came for the Christmas party, but I feel like a bit of a fraud.'

'A fraud? Do you? Why's that?' Tess asked loudly.

He held her blue gaze as he answered. 'Because it seems strange to be at a staff Christmas party before I've even started work.'

'It's a good casual way to settle in. Once you're here working you'll be surprised how busy the days are on the island,' Eliza said with a smile. 'How long have you been living on Hamilton island?'

'Oh, I come and go,' he said. 'I've just come back from Ningaloo in the west. I was looking for a friend who was supposed to be over there.' When Tess's cheeks coloured, he knew that she was aware of the bum steer her brothers had given him. Good, maybe she'd realise how determined he had been to find her, and maybe she'd wonder why.

He'd searched for her nonstop over the past two years, and he had vowed that he would not give up until he found her. He knew what she'd done for him, and he wanted her to know that.

Zac knew her well, and he knew to tread softly. But he was going to talk to Tess tonight, because he was worried she would take off now that he'd found her.

'When do you start work, *Monty?*' Tess stared at him. There was a hardness in her gaze that had never been there before.

'We don't have a date yet. Rafe said he would let me know. But I will come over tomorrow.' He held her gaze and neither looked away until Eliza spoke.

The completion of the pool won't be far off.' Eliza looked at them curiously. The undercurrent between them must be obvious. 'The concrete has to cure for four weeks and Dylan's organised for the landscaping to be done in that time. The bar will be built before the pool is filled, so there's going to be plenty for you to do. Anyway enough of work. Who'd like another drink?' Eliza jumped up and grabbed Philippe's hand. 'And a dance, please, my love.'

'Tess?' He waited until Sienna and Danny got up to dance too.

She looked at him and raised her eyebrows, and again Zac was struck by her new confidence. 'Yes?'

'Come for a walk with me? I want to talk to you.'

'I don't want to talk to you, though, so that's a no.'

'Tess—'

'No, *Zac.* You listen to me. I don't owe you anything. I don't have to talk to you, and I don't want to listen to you.'

He ran his hand through his hair, frustrated. Short of kidnapping her, Tess wasn't going to let him explain. His voice was low and he tried to keep it level. 'Do you know how many months I've spent looking for you? Do you know how worried I am that you'll disappear again before I can talk to you.'

'That's all very nice to hear, but I'm not going anywhere. You've chased me from one career, and I've developed a lot of self-preservation skills since then, so I'm not going anywhere. That being said, I really can't see the need for you to stay and wait around to "talk" to me. So if that's your only reason for taking on a job on Pentecost Island—which I find ridiculous—you might as well leave now and not come back.' She sat back and folded her arms, her eyes challenging him. 'What sort of job is it, anyway? Are you providing financial advice to the guests as they lie around the pool?' The sarcasm in her voice stung, but he bit his tongue.

Zac had spent so much time and energy trying to find her, that snarky comment really pissed him off. But despite the anger that gripped him, he couldn't stop looking at her. He'd thought she was beautiful before—inside and out—but with her chin in the air and her eyes wide as she stared him down, he thought she'd never looked so vital, and full of life, her eyes snapping at him.

'You *have* matured, Tess. And no, I'll not be giving financial advice. Like you, I've reinvented myself. What happened to you was a wakeup call for me. It made me realise what's important in life.'

'I'm not interested in any of that, Zac. I only have one question for you.' She leaned forward and keep her voice low. They were still alone at the table, but she obviously didn't want their argument to be overheard.

He looked past her and was dismayed to see the two couples at the table across from them all paying close interest, obviously intrigued by their interaction. Zac leaned closer to her, and took her hand, speaking quickly. 'The group at the table behind you are very interested in what we're doing, so I'd suggest that we both chill a bit, unless you want to be the centre of attention. Smile at me, be nice and I'll answer anything you want to know.'

As he watched, Tess relaxed, her shoulders loosened, and her chin lowered. He kept smiling at her and flicked a quick glance to the other table as one of the two couples got up to dance.

'Okay, it's cool now,' he said.

But as the couple walked past the table the woman paused and spoke to Tess, after flicking a curious glance at Zac. 'Thanks again for giving me an early mark, Tess. I appreciated it. We'—she patted her stomach—'even had a quick nap.'

Tess was on her best behaviour now. She smiled across at Zac. 'Zac, have you met Nell and Nat?'

He stood, reached over and shook the guy's hand. 'No. I haven't. Nice to meet you, Monty's the nickname.'

'Welcome,' Nell said, but Nat looked at him curiously. 'I think we've met before, Monty? Haven't we?'

Zac shook his head. 'I don't think so.'

Nat frowned. 'I think I've seen you around on Hamo.'

'That's probably it.'

Nat took Nell's hand and they headed to the dance floor.

Zac sat down and turned back to Tess. Her smile had gone and she looked past him over his shoulder. 'Your question?'

'How did you find me?'

Chapter 18
Pippa

Tonight was the first time I'd ever seen Rafe cry, and he broke my heart. He was trying to comfort *me*, and I was the one who did most of the comforting, although I did cry with him.

'I thought I was pregnant, but I hadn't been to the doctor. I was going to tell you this week and then go over to Hamo to the doctor. I've had no symptoms at all. I've been Googling but I don't—didn't—have any of the things they said I probably would.' Tears pricked at my eyes again as I realised I could probably stop looking for any changes in my body.

We were lying together on our bed. I'd had to talk Rafe out of putting me in the boat and going straight over to the medical centre on Hamilton Island. The cramps had eased, and the shock of knowing I had been pregnant, and had now miscarried had exhausted me.

He lay on his side, his hand smoothing my hair gently. His eyes were sad, but I could still see the love there as he soothed me. Guilt hit me in the chest and I swallowed.

'I'm going to tell you the truth, Rafe,' I whispered. 'We promised each other we would be honest, didn't we? But I wasn't.'

'We did.' His hand stilled. 'It's okay, love. Just lie there and rest.'

'No. I want to tell you, so you know. I was scared. More than bloody scared. I was terrified, because I didn't know if I wanted to be pregnant, and I knew how much you wanted us to have a baby quickly. I didn't know how to tell you that. And when I missed my monthlies, I didn't want to get your hopes up, but more than anything, if I told you, it would make it real and I didn't know how I felt about that. But now I feel guilty because I didn't tell you how I felt. I'm sorry. I've let you down.' I started to cry again.

'No, Pip.'

He made a strangled sound and lifted his hand, but I put my mine on his.

'Hear me out. I was worried I would be like my mother, and that I wouldn't love our child, like she never loved me.' I found my tissue and dabbed at my eyes and blew my nose. 'She loved my dad, and she didn't have enough love to go around. Aunty Vi told me that wasn't normal, and that my mum had other issues too. Issues that I was too young to see. And then I worried that I had those issues too. I was so worried, my head was a mess and I wasn't game to tell you I thought I was pregnant and I would have to come to terms with how I felt.' My voice shook again. 'And I didn't know how I felt, apart from being bloody scared. It was the worst I'd ever felt in my life. Even worse than when my dad died.'

'Babe, I want what you want. And if you don't want to have children, that's the way it will be. As long as I've got you in my life, that's all I need.'

I shook my head from side to side. 'No. Losing this little one, even though he or she would have only been a couple of months old—

no bigger than a jelly bean I read the other day—has broken my heart and made me realise that I *can* do this. That baby was part of us. He or she was us. A physical person that we created out of our love. I *can* do this. I *want* to do it. If I struggle, you'll be there by my side. You are the one constant in my life. The one person I can trust. That's how much I love you, Rafe.' My voice thickened and more tears rolled down my cheeks.

Rafe rolled over and held me close. His cheek was wet against mine. 'There is nothing more in my life than you. I love you, Phillipa.'

'I wondered if he somehow knew that I had doubts and that's why he didn't want to stay,' I sobbed.

'Oh sweetheart, don't blame yourself.' His voice broke.

I buried my face in his neck and cried with the man I loved with my heart and soul.

Chapter 19

Tess rose before sunrise the next morning and climbed the hill so she could watch the sun rise over the ocean. Over the past few months she'd loved standing on the hill above the resort and watching the dawn lighten the sky. The sky would be dark when she sat on her favourite rock, and then it would lighten and that gorgeous apricot colour would creep up from the sea, until the sky turned gold and red and pink. Watching the sunrise had always soothed her but she'd let the habit slip lately as she got busier with her job in the office.

She needed its calming influence today. Seeing Zac last night had rocked Tess's world. Sitting beside him, and looking at him as he spoke to the others had been hard. The attraction that she had felt for him two years ago hadn't lessened one bit—even though she knew he was not to be trusted. Her body had betrayed her, and all she could think of was how his skin had felt beneath her fingertips, his lips on hers, his breath tickling her ear as he talked to her. Her body had forgotten the confusion, the sadness and the bewilderment, and the unbearable betrayal when she'd realised Zac had believed the worst of her.

She had been young—even though she was only two years older now than when she'd fallen in love with him, when she had spent one glorious month hoping he was her future—Tess felt about twenty years older now.

In maturity and common sense

anyway. It had been a very quick way to learn self-confidence, and to be self-reliant.

Dad had been right all along; she should have listened to him. Zac Montgomery was way out of her league. He'd come from a different world to her; he had different standards and values. It was about the dollar. It had been a good wake up call for Theresa Anderson.

A goat bleated up the hill and brought her back to the present. She was on the first shift in the office this morning, and as soon as the sun had cleared the horizon, she'd jog back down the hill, have a quick shower, and grab some breakfast.

At least she didn't have to worry about running into Zac this morning because he'd said he was going back to Hamo last night with Jiminy. After talking to Eliza, she'd made her excuses and left the party.

She'd run through the forest, remembering the night she'd run through The Rocks and got lost.

Mum had cried when they'd said goodbye at Central Station the next morning and even Ted had hugged her.

It had been two years since she'd seen them. Zac could shoulder the blame for the loss of her family too.

The first launch wasn't over until ten so Tess knew she had some respite. With a bit of luck, they wouldn't cross paths. She'd stay in the office between the launch coming each day. If he did appear in the office, she'd go in the back room and Nell could deal with him.

With a yawn, Tess lifted her face to the first warm rays of the sun. Any sleep she'd managed to snatch had been broken by dreams of Zac holding her. She took a deep breath and held it, letting the serenity fill her before she headed back down to the old house. There were some decisions to make.

As her former boss, Tess was concerned that Zac would share her past job history with Pippa, and that her position—her traineeship—would be compromised. While she kept that in her mind, and how he had immediately thought she had done the wrong thing, and not given her a chance to defend herself, she was able to stay strong, and push away the attraction that he damn well still held for her.

How the hell had he found her?

Loose stones slipped beneath her shoes as Tess turned and made her way down the hill. She would be strong, because she would not give up her job. If Zac raised anything with Pippa, she would pull out the one ace she had up her sleeve. The one that she had not spoken of two years ago, because she had foolishly tried to protect Zac.

He hadn't even sought her out. She had been tried and found guilty by the CEO, but worst of all, Zac had believed that she had done the wrong thing.

With a determined grunt. Tess picked up her pace and as soon as the hill levelled out, she began to jog, forcing herself to go faster, and enjoying the pain it caused. While ever she was dealing with that, she would not think about the past and Zac Montgomery.

I can do it.

By the time she reached the site of the new pool Tess was a lather of perspiration and her breath was ragged.

***

It had been well after midnight when Zac got back to his boat in the marina; he'd lingered talking to Jiminy, not wanting any of the staff who'd travelled back to Hamo to see him go to his vessel at the middle wharf. Once he was in the master suite he found it impossible to sleep. Spending the night in Tess's company had brought back the great times they had spent together two years ago, and the strong feelings that he'd held for her.

The love that he still felt for

her.

Those feelings had never left him and had fed his determination to find her. It had been a long and hard road, and her family had been impossible. He knew when Reeza's brothers had told him she was in Western Australia that they'd been lying, but he wasn't prepared to risk it, just in case she was there. He admired them for respecting her privacy even though it had made his job of finding her bloody nigh impossible.

He would never forget the moment when he'd spotted the photo on the noticeboard in the staff quarters on his boat. Even with her short blonde hair, he'd recognised Reeza straight away. The relief had been overwhelming, but a photo was only the start. When he'd asked about it he'd discovered it had been taken about three months ago in a bar on Hamilton Island.

The last time he'd been at Hamo. He shook his head as he realised she'd been there on the same island, and he hadn't known.

The problem was that when he'd seen the photo they'd been moored off Exmouth in Western Australia. The staff and crew had been surprised when he'd told them they were going straight back to the east coast. They'd only been in this incredible location for a week; it had taken three weeks to cruise around the Top End and reach Exmouth.

'Now?' Marty, his captain—and the one who'd pinned the photo on the board—had screwed his face up. 'You want to go back to the east coast now? We've only just got here, Zac.'

'Yes, humour me, please, Marty.' Zac gripped the photo in his hand and stared down at it. 'Now tell me the name of the bar where this was taken? And when?'

The photo was of his skipper with his arm around a dark-haired woman, but all Zac was interested in was the woman behind the bar. She was looking at the camera.

It was *Reeza.* Working in a bar, for fuck's sake.

He knew it was her. He was as sure of that as he was that the sun would set over the sea this afternoon. He had been looking for her for almost two years hounding her family, and following false leads.

Whoever would have guessed that she would appear in the background of a random photo pinned up on the staff announcement board of his cruiser?

Marty took the photo from his hand and frowned. 'It was taken in the Bristolian Bar a couple of months ago, the week you flew back to Sydney when *Myr* was being serviced at Hamo.

Zac had rolled his eyes and groaned. He'd left the boat and the crew at Hamilton Island to fly back and beg Reeza's family one last time, and that's when they'd told him she was in the west. He'd come back and they'd headed west two weeks later. She'd been on the island the whole time.

'Cindy was looking for a job on the boats, and we agreed to meet at the bar that night. I know it was two months ago, because she had to be back in Cairns to go back to work at the end of September.'

'Okay. And can you tell me anything about the girl behind the bar? The one in the photo.' Zac had taken the photo back from Marty and stared at him.

'I'm sorry, mate. I never even noticed her. What's the big deal?'

'The big deal is we're going back to Hamilton Island. Now. Tell the crew to pull up anchor and get moving.'

'Ah, boss? Some of them are onshore at Exmouth.'

'Well, get them back to the boat as quickly as you can and then we're going. Thank you.'

The two weeks it took to cruise back to the east coast were the longest of Zac's life. They needed to plot the route so they reached ports to refuel in the daylight and his frustration had built as they'd had to spend a night in Broome, Darwin, Cooktown, and Townsville. He'd thought about flying back, but told himself it had been two years, and he would wait, and think about his approach.

If indeed she was still there.

He knew Marty, his captain, thought he was mad, and maybe he had been. But now he was back in the Whitsundays, he'd tracked Reeza down from the bar to Pentecost Island and discovered she now called herself Tess. Then his first stroke of good luck arrived; his mate, Rafe lived on Pentecost Island and his wife ran the resort. He'd talked to Rafe— they'd been friends since they'd met when Zac had first come to the islands. He'd told him the whole story and asked him to keep it to himself, and Rafe had come up with the idea of a job on the island.

Zac gave up trying to sleep and went up to the deck. *Myr*, his forty metre yacht, had been his escape after he had walked out of the bank, the week after Reeza had been accused of theft. It had taken three months to have the luxury yacht delivered, and he'd lived on board ever since. If it hadn't been for his lack of success finding Reeza, he could have settled into his new life. The life of his dreams. But the worry of what had happened to her had refused to leave him.

Zac had discovered the truth within hours; it hadn't taken much. Reeza had been set up, and he was determined to find her and make amends. And support her. But to his dismay, she had disappeared that night, and had proved impossible to find.

Myr had been the realisation of his dream, to live on the water. But that dream had turned to dust, and when he hadn't been able to find Reeza, he'd taken little pleasure from the new life he'd tried to live. His search had become an obsession and Zac knew he couldn't go on like that forever. The trip to Exmouth was going to be his last attempt.

He lay back and looked at the night sky. The velvet background was black and dotted with millions of stars. The only sound was the slap of the water on the hull, and he tried to focus on what he'd do.

He had one shot with Reeza. *Tess,* he reminded himself. And he would not stuff up.

The warm breeze played on his

face and Zac closed his eyes and drifted off to sleep as the stars moved across the sky.

Chapter 20

When Tess heard voices from behind the huts where the formwork for the pool was being built she decided to have a look at the pool area. Eliza and Pippa were excited about the development and by all accounts, the infinity pool was going to be pretty spectacular. Tess hadn't been to the site since the hole had been dug last week.

The view from the pool site looked out over an expanse of the Passage where there were no other islands to impede the view. Just endless clear blue water and sky. The pool design had platforms holding eight day beds. The view was framed by two well-established palm trees on the edge of the shore. Apparently Eliza had sourced some timber-framed day beds which would give privacy options to guests as they visited the pool. Their plan was to have a bar at the island edge of the pool, and to make it another activity hub along with the main bar and restaurant.

Tess sighed; she really wanted Zac—or Monty, or whoever he was these days— to be gone. She loved her job and her life on Pentecost Island, and she didn't want to have to start over. But if he made it too hard, she would go. No matter how attracted to him she still was, she would never forgive Zac for not supporting her on that dreadful day.

Tess turned along the garden-edged path that led to the pool area. Even though she knew Zac was coming here to meet with Pippa and Eliza today, it was too early for him to have arrived yet and Jiminy wouldn't arrive with the day's passengers for another three hours yet. She lifted her arm and wiped the perspiration from her face as she stepped out of the rainforest. Even though it was just after six, the heat was building. She followed the voices and when she stepped past the last hut on the waterfront, she drew a quick breath.

He'd lied. Zac hadn't left the island last night at all. He was standing on the beach below the pool talking to Danny Riccardo.

Why was she not surprised? Whatever he did he couldn't be trusted, and he hadn't changed. He had to call the shots. She'd fallen for it once, but she'd learned a lot since then. She had been a naive young woman who'd fallen for a sophisticated man with a smooth spiel. The events that had led to the end of her career had hurt, but the way Zac had used her had hurt a hundred times more. Tess stepped back slowly into the glade so they wouldn't see her, but she was too late.

'Morning, Tess,' Zac called cheerily and Danny echoed the greeting.

'I saw you up on the hill as Renzo and I came into the bay,' Danny said. 'You're keen to jog at this time of the year.'

'Gets the blood pumping,' Tess said as she walked over to them, but was careful to keep her eyes on Danny, and not look at Zac.

'I didn't know you jogged, Tess,' Zac said.

'Why would you?' she said sharply and Danny looked at her

curiously.

Zac shrugged and there was silence for a moment.

'Did you stay the night on the island after all, *Monty*?' she couldn't resist asking.

'No, I came over on my boat half an hour ago. Danny told me last night before I left with Jiminy that he'd be here early, so I decided to come over early too,' he said.

Tess widened her eyes, but was determined not to comment. *His boat?* He'd achieved his dream and had a boat?

'I haven't had a chance to see Pippa and Eliza yet, but Renzo managed to double the formwork crew today and we're set.' Danny laughed. 'Sometimes it helps to be Italian.'

'Why's that?' Tess asked.

'Half of our cousins are concreters,' Danny said with a grin.

'Do you want me to let Pippa and Eliza know you're looking for them when I get to the office? I start work at seven.'

'That's early enough, thanks. The guys won't be here until nine-thirty. They were driving down from Ingham last night.' Danny nodded. 'If you could get a message to Eliza, that'd be great. Pippa's not here. We passed Rafe's boat heading to Hamo on the way over, and Pippa and Rafe were both on it.'

Tess frowned. 'That's early.'

'Yeah, I wondered myself where they were going.' Danny said. 'Anyway, if Eliza's here that's fine.' He turned to Zac. 'I've got to go up the hill and help Renzo at the new staff apartments for an hour or so. Have a look around, and see what you reckon. It'll be good to have another opinion. See you later, Tess.'

Tess froze as she realised she was going to be left alone with Zac. She turned away. 'I have to go and get ready for work.'

'Tess, wait. Please. We need to talk. And this is a perfect opportunity. There's no one around, and we can be frank.' She looked down as he touched her arm, but Zac must have thought better of it and he lifted his hand straight away.

She put her hands on her hips. 'I can be frank all right. I don't want to talk to you, I don't want you on the island, and I have no idea what you're doing here.'

'I'm here because I have a job, and the bonus is I get to see you.

266

I'd like to make amends, Tess, and spend some time with you and get to know you all over again.'

'Make amends? That's a joke.' She stared at Zac, and for the first time Tess noticed the shadows beneath his eyes.

'I'm serious. But we need to talk.'

'We're just going around in circles here, Zac. The sooner you realise I don't want to talk to you the better. I don't want to be in your company.' Tess had no idea what skills Zac could bring to the island. 'What sort of job are you doing? There's not much of a demand for investment bankers here.'

'I don't do that anymore,' he said quietly.

'So what are you doing here?'

'I'm here to see you.'

'You've wasted your time.' She shook her head slowly as she stared at him, 'And you have a boat too?'

'I do.'

'What sort of boat?'

'The boat I came over on is a small runabout but it's big enough to get me from Hamilton Island to here, or to the mainland.' He stared at her, and she found it hard to look away. 'It's moored at the jetty if you want to see it.'

'No. I'm not interested. I was just curious.' She tipped her head to the side and held his blue-eyed gaze, ignoring the ripple that tugged at her. 'So you left the bank and followed your dream?'

***

Zac had been surprised, but very pleased, when Tess walked out of the glade when he was talking to Danny. And happy. It was the first time he'd seen her in running clothes and he was surprised at how fit and toned she was. Over the past two years, she'd changed in many ways; she had matured and her self-confidence was obvious. Her skin had more colour and she looked healthy.

But the change in her had not lessened the strong attraction he felt; it was still there as strong as ever.

The problem was that Tess was looking at him as though he was something that had crawled from beneath a rock. But her comment about following his dream encouraged him; maybe she wasn't as resistant to him as he'd thought. Maybe it was a front she was putting up.

Whatever it was, Zac knew to tread carefully.

'I did follow my dream,' he said. 'I just have one more thing to do and I will be very content with my life.'

She didn't ask what that was, but she stood there sizing him up. When Zac had left the bank, he'd embraced a more physical life. He'd joined a gym and a swimming club, and built his fitness and taken on a variety of outdoor activities. The only thing he couldn't understand was why it had taken him so long to realise how his quality of life had been lacking those fifteen years he'd worked at the bank.

'You look well, anyway. I have to go to work now.' Tess turned away and Zac went to speak, and ask her to see him after work, but something told him not to push.

'Have a good day.' Turning away and not watching Tess walk away was hard, but Zac was beginning to realise how carefully he was going to have to approach this. He'd been naive, kidding himself that all he had to do was find Tess, apologise, and all would be right. He'd focused on the search and on finding her, and not given any thought to the fact that she wouldn't be receptive.

'You're a fool,' he told himself. Zac knew he needed help; Rafe knew the situation and was a level-headed guy. He'd head up to the house when they got back to the island and use him as a sounding board.

And maybe Pippa too.

Maybe she knew the new Tess, and that approach might work.

The last thing Zac wanted was
to have Tess disappear again.

Chapter 21

'Damn it.' Tess shook her hand and put it up to her mouth. She'd shut the filing cabinet too hard and jammed her thumb.

'Coffee time?' Nell asked looking at her over the top of her glasses. Nell had been humming and singing and smiling all morning, the direct opposite to Tess's grumpy mood.

'Sure is. I didn't sleep too well.' Tess smoothed her hands down her black shorts. 'Would you like a herbal tea?' Nell had given up coffee while she was pregnant.

'That'd be good, thanks. There's some peppermint teabags in the kitchen. Now that all the checkouts are done, we've got an hour before Jiminy arrives with the next lot. You and I are going to go out to the veranda and have a chat.'

Tess's stomach clenched; she jerked her head up and stared at Nell. Had Zac already told them about her past? 'Why, have I done something wrong?' Once she would have waited to be told, but these days with her new confidence, she was on the front foot and she challenged.

'God, no. Don't be silly. I want to talk to you because I'm worried about you. You've been like a cat on a hot tin roof all morning.'

Sweet relief loosened Tess's limbs and she flopped into the desk chair. 'Sorry, I'm a bit touchy this morning. I thought I must have been a bit short with one of the guests or something.'

Or something. That the girls on the island had found out that she supposedly stole almost a million dollars two years ago. Tess had never found out what the upshot of it all had been. One minute she was going to be arrested, then the charges were dropped, the media came baying for her blood, and she took off.

And not one call from Zac.

Total silence. No contact. He'd believed the worst of her, and had never even realised what she had done to save his skin. She could have blurted out that that he had been with him on that Friday night when she allegedly had been in the bank stealing money, but she had thought of Zac and his position. A lot of good that had done.

And now it appeared he'd left the bank, and had a boat.

And he'd turned up at the same island where she was

beginning to find her happiness.

Why was he here? It seemed Zac had known she was already here, and she had no idea how that had happened. He'd been waiting for her in the glade to come from the office.

Tess frowned. Was there someone on the island she couldn't trust? There was something not quite right with that scenario.

Nell's laugh pulled her out of her thoughts. 'No, quite the opposite. I was wishing I had your patience when you were dealing with that grumpy old bloke who checked out last. The one who wouldn't let his wife say a word. Every time she went to speak he would make that awful clicking noise in his throat.'

'Mr Gray? He reminded me of my dad. He was easy enough to

deal with, but I did feel sorry for his wife.' Tess laughed too. 'Poor lady was too soft. My mum developed a thick skin over the years. She's louder than Dad is now. I'll go and get that cuppa. Do you want some morning tea with it? Cherry brought up some lemon drizzle cake.'

'I shouldn't, but yes please. If I'm going to look fat at my wedding'—she shot a cheeky glance at Tess—'I want it to be all baby, not too much fat from cake.'

'Wedding? What wedding?'

'Our wedding beside the pool as soon as it's finished.' Nell held her hand out and Tess felt mean. She'd been so damn cranky she hadn't even noticed the diamond ring on Nell's left hand all morning. 'You're the first to know. Officially, anyway. Pippa and Tamsin knew it was going to happen, but Nat surprised me.'

Tears stung Tess's eyes. 'Really? When did this happen?'

'Last night after the party. I knew Nat had the ring and I thought he was going to wait for Christmas to ask me, but he took me down to the beach and popped the question last night.'

Tess jumped up and hugged Nell. 'That is such good news. You've improved my mood!'

'Can I ask why it needed improving?' Nell asked quietly.

'Just some past worries resurfaced. But I'm fine. I'll get through it.'

'If you ever need a shoulder . . .'

'Thanks, Nell. I'm all good. But I appreciate it. One of the things I love about being on Pentecost is the warm friendship I've been offered.'

'We're a pretty special place.' Nell stretched and rubbed her back. 'Now go and get our drinks and I'll finish up here and we'll sit on the veranda. There's about sixteen new guests coming in on the morning boat, I think.'

'Yes, seven couples and two singles,' Tess confirmed as she headed out the door 'And they're all here for the week. Which will save a bit of checking in and out. I like it when they all arrive at the same time.'

'Me too.'

Ten minutes later, Tess carried a tray out to the veranda where Nell was sitting gazing over the bay. The sky was a deep cloudless blue and the water was barely ruffled by the slight breeze that blew from the north. The azure water was dotted with white sails as yachts tried to catch the very occasional puff of wind.

'Sometimes I pinch myself to believe I really live here. It looks smooth out on the water today,' Nell commented as she reached for the cup of tea on the tray. 'Have you had a chance to go out for a sail since you've been up here?'

'No, I haven't. I worked long hours on Hamo when I was there, and now I'm happy to chill here on Pentecost when I'm not working.'

'Where did you live before you came to the islands, Tess?' Nell's voice was casual, but Tess knew she was digging. But it wasn't curiosity for gossip. She knew Nell was concerned.

'On our family orchard west of Sydney.'

'Nice. We'll have to organise a trip to Whitehaven Beach for you.'

'One day,' Tess said. 'There's so much to do here. But I have plenty of time.'

'When the staff accommodation is built and the pool area is done, there'll be a bit of a break.'

Tess raised her eyebrows. 'You really think so?'

'Probably not, knowing Pippa,' Nell said. 'And I think Eliza is her clone. They'll have some other project on the go. They are both full of ideas.'

'And energy.' Tess lifted one of the cake plates from the tray and handed it to Nell. 'I only cut two small pieces. I'm so excited to hear there's a wedding coming up. There's always something happening here.'

'There is, but it's been a quiet

morning apart from checkouts. I've been waiting for Eliza and Pippa to come into the office, but there's been no sign of them.'

'Pippa and Rafe went to Hamo early, and Eliza's over at the pool site with Danny. Apparently the pool is going to be finished a lot earlier than they thought.' Tess sat opposite Nell.

Nell put her tea down and clapped her hands. 'Really? That's fantastic. We might even get a February wedding, and I won't be too huge.'

'When's the baby due?' Tess asked as she reached for her slice of cake.

'Ours at the end of June and Tamsin in mid- April. The babies will have a playmate.'

'Lots of excitement coming up. A wedding and two babies.'

'And our new houses are starting to be built as soon as the pool and staff accommodation are done. With the birth, a new baby and a move to our home, I'm hoping that you'll be able to take over the office while I take a few months off.'

'Really? Oh yes, that would be—' Tess cut her words off.

'That would be?' Nell looked at her curiously.

'I *think* that will be fine,' Tess said quietly.

'You're not going to run away with that gorgeous Monty and leave us, are you?'

Tess's face heated. 'Oh, God no.'

That's the last thing she'd do.

She lifted her head and held Nell's gaze. 'Thank you. I would be pleased to look after the office while you are off. I'll stay here as long as there's a job for me. Thank you for having faith in me.' Tess took a deep breath. 'You don't know how much that trust means to me.'

She would not let Zac chase her away. This was her place. Whatever his secret was, when she agreed to talk to him, she would keep, and he could keep quiet about their past.

'Are you sure you don't want to talk about what's bothering you, hun?' Nell asked.

'Thanks, Nell. That's lovely of you, but it involves someone else, and I agreed not to discuss it.'

Secrets! What was he on about?

'Fair enough. But I assume it's our new lifeguard?' Nell put her hand up. 'I won't ask anymore. I picked up on the tension last night. Just know if you ever need an ear, I'm happy to listen.'

Tess's eyes widened and she couldn't help the grin that was tugging at her lips. 'Did you say lifeguard?'

Nell nodded. 'Apparently Monty is our pool lifeguard, and new barman. For the pool bar and the restaurant bar. It was organised pretty quickly. I still don't have any employment stuff or tax forms through. Remind me to ask Pippa about them.'

'That will be *interesting*.' Tess stood and picked up the tray. 'And that's all I'm going to say. Being a lifeguard is interesting, I mean.' As she looked out over the water, Rafe's boat motored into the bay. 'Look here's Rafe and Pippa now.'

'Are you okay here? I'd like to

go over and meet them at the wharf.' Nell waggled her left hand. 'After I show them this, I'll chase up those forms for Monty.'

'Don't rush, we've still got a while before Jiminy arrives with the check ins.'

Chapter 22
Pippa

Rafe had one arm around my shoulder and held me close as he kept his other hand on the helm. He steered the motorboat into the jetty in his usual careful way and I glanced at the small runabout that was tied up to the other side.

'I wonder who that belongs to.'

'Zac,' Rafe said as the boat slid in alongside the jetty. When I went to step onto the wharf to help with the ropes as I always did, he shook his head and grabbed my hand. 'No, you stay right there. Here comes Zac now. He can do it. You're going to take it easy for a couple of days.'

'Nell's coming through the glade too. Rafe?' I looked up at his shadowed eyes, and my heart broke all over again. I had to be strong in front of Nell. She would guess something was wrong. I was about to put on the best act of my life. 'I don't want to tell anyone about the miscarriage. Okay? I don't want to upset Nell and Tam.'

'Okay, if anyone asks, I took you over for breakfast.'

'Thank you. Also is it Zac or Monty? I'm confused.'

'I'll tell you the story when we get up to the house. Probably Monty's best for now because that's what he's asked to be known as.'

My appointment at the medical centre had been quick. The doctor had confirmed the miscarriage and booked me into the hospital on the mainland for a D&C next week. She had been lovely and told me how common miscarriage was and not to be too concerned.

'When you're pregnant again, the anxiety and sometimes mixed emotions you feel about the pregnancy are completely normal. Don't be frightened by your feelings, Phillipa. And also, it's really important that you try not to be hard on yourself. Some women feel guilty that they may have let their partner down, that's not the case. There's usually a reason for miscarriage. Come and see me in a couple of weeks, okay?'

I'd nodded, holding back my tears, and went back to Rafe in the waiting room.

I swallowed as Nell walked across the sand. Tam's pregnancy was very obvious already, but Nell only had a tiny bump so far; if you didn't know she was pregnant, you'd never notice.

'Morning, Pip. Hi, Rafe. Where

have you two been off to so early?'

'Breakfast,' I said with a smile. 'Rafe offered to spoil me before the day began.'

Nell laughed. 'Pippa Rendell, your husband spoils you twenty-four seven.'

I managed to look nonchalant, and wave a lazy hand. 'And so he should. I'm worth it.'

'Hi Monty.' I turned as Rafe's friend walked along the wharf and stood behind Nell.

'Sorry to interrupt, but can I come up to the house and see you both sometime this morning?'

'Sure,' I said. 'Come up now.' It would give me an out with Nell before I gave into the tears I could feel building again. 'Nell, did you need me for something?' I asked as Rafe threw the line to Monty to secure us to the jetty.

Nell smiled and shook her head before she lifted her hand. 'No, nothing important.' Her smile was incandescent, and I waited for her to finish. 'Just wanted to tell you Nat asked me to marry him and we're engaged, and to ask you if we can get married by the pool in February.'

My mouth dropped and I moved to the swim platform at the back of the boat to step off. Normally I would have climbed over the side but I was feeling a bit fragile. My throat clogged as I walked to Nell and when I reached her, I burst into tears. I grabbed her in a big hug as the tears ran down my face. 'Oh, Nellie, that is wonderful.'

Eventually I stepped back, unsurprised to see tears in Nell's eyes. I cleared my throat. 'Did you say February?'

She nodded and wiped her eyes. 'If we can book a wedding in.'

I linked my arm through hers. 'Do you want to come up for a cuppa?'

'Later. I have to get back to the office now. Tess'll need a hand with the check ins. We've got a few in today. A big changeover.'

I swallowed. 'I think this calls for drinks at sunset. Just you and me and Tam. Is that okay?'

'Sure is. All for one drinks, hey? Just the three of us.'

'Yes, just the three of us,' I said, my voice husky.

Nell smiled through her tears. 'Sound good to me. I'll go over to the restaurant and tell Tam at lunchtime. And before I forget, Danny wants to see you and Eliza as soon as you can get over there.'

Normal life had returned, and I had to get used to it. My universe had shifted, but Rafe was still the centre of it. I was really happy for Nell, but my smile was sad as I walked across to Rafe.

He put his arm around me. 'Okay, love?'

'I'm okay.'

Chapter 23

Tess

Check in time was hectic like it always was. The new arrivals were keen to get to their huts and explore the island, and Tess and Nell were keen to process them quickly. They handed out the brochures that Pippa had produced about the Red Wall walk—with a warning about the feral goats—and took bookings for the restaurant sittings tonight.

Just after one, Tess sat back with a sigh of relief. 'I think we're done, Nell.'

'I've never had so many questions asked,' Nell said. 'They were a curious lot. Especially that rock climbing group.'

'Mine all booked into the day spa. That took ages,' Tess said. 'Sienna is going to be really busy for the next few days. Did I hear there's another therapist coming to work on the island?'

'Yes. Pippa's interviewing an Irish girl Sienna met at her course, but not until next week. And there's no room in the house for more staff so I guess if she's suitable she won't start until the staff accommodation is ready.'

'So she won't be here to help with these bookings.' Tess closed the check-in program on her screen, and asked casually. 'Is that why Monty isn't staying on the island?'

Nell stood and stretched, and giggled when her stomach rumbled. 'Probably. Although we have so many staff coming over on Jiminy's launch these days, I think he's going to increase to two trips each way every day soon.' Nell covered her mouth as she yawned. 'Do you want to have your lunch break first?'

'No, you go first. I've got a few things to finish up here,' Tess said. Plus she had no desire to go for her usual midday walk and risk bumping into Zac.

'Thanks. I'll be back in an hour. Do you want me to order you some lunch from the restaurant while I'm down there?'

'No, I'm fine thanks. I'll just make a sandwich in the kitchen here.'

Nell nodded and was gone quickly. Tess sat back and stretched her arms above her head, feeling the best she had since last night when she'd bumped into Zac. The busy morning had put things in perspective for her. As much as she still had feelings for Zac she could put her head down and do her work, and keep to herself. At night, she had study to do, and didn't have to socialise with the staff group and risk seeing him. Not that that was likely to happen because he apparently was living over on Hamo.

The only thing that worried her was why he was here. She knew he was here because she was—and his insistence that they had to talk—confirmed that.

But why?

If it was about what happened at the bank, Tess knew she wasn't strong enough to deal with that.

Not yet. The experience and the very brief run in with the media had traumatised her, along with the knowledge that Zac hadn't even bothered to contact her.

If he was here to try and resurrect a relationship, she knew she definitely wasn't strong enough for that. It made her angry that she was still so attracted to him.

She'd put her head down, avoid the pool when he was at work, and ignore him if he came on her radar, and get on with her life. Hopefully he'd take the hint and go back to wherever he came from.

And she would forget about how incredibly sexy he looked these days with his longer hair and buff body. For an almost forty-year-old guy, he was hot.

Tess walked out to the veranda and stared at the water. Strangely, she had found being near the sea was soothing. Growing up on the orchard had meant very little time by the ocean, and she hadn't experienced that way of relaxing before. When she'd commented to Tamsin one night how the water calmed her, Tam had tipped her head to the side and observed her carefully.

'Cancerian?'

Tess had nodded. 'Yes, I was a June baby.'

'Water is your element. I'll do your astrological chart for you one night.'

Tess had smiled. 'I don't think I believe in all that stuff.'

'Oh, girlfriend, trust me. You'll be very surprised. Pippa was the most sceptical of all when I did hers, and you ask her how it all turned out. You watch, I guarantee she'll be pregnant by the end of this year.'

'Okay, I'll get you to do it one night. Could be fun.'

'An eye-opener too.' Tam had

smiled and looked at her curiously. 'It might pull up some things you don't like.'

Tess had grinned. 'If it does I can pull up my big girl panties and move on.'

But that was before Zac Montgomery had turned up on the island. Until she knew why he was here, she wasn't going to settle. Tess leaned down and put her elbows on the railing and propped her chin in her hands. From here she could just see the wharf at the base of the hill where Rafe's black boat was moored. There was an unfamiliar small runabout toed up on the other side. She guessed that was Zac's boat. A long way from the dream cruiser he'd talked about.

She wondered why he'd left the bank.

Maybe she would have that talk with him, and find out what his secret was. He'd never said what he'd meant when he'd said, "I need you to keep a secret." But she'd guessed it was about him going by the name of Monty. But Tess had no idea why he would have changed his name.

With a shrug, she went back to the office and sat down. If she refused to listen to him and whatever he wanted to say, she would be on tenterhooks waiting.

She wouldn't seek him out, but next time she saw him, she'd agree to listen. Then, not only could she make a plan of action, but with any luck, he'd jump in his little runabout, go back to Hamilton Island—which was still too close for her peace of mind—and leave her alone,

By the time Nell came back to relieve her for her lunch, Tess had decided there was no point in putting off *the talk* any longer.

Chapter 24
Zac

Zac sat out on the balcony at Pippa and Rafe's house overlooking the wharf. He'd agreed to tell Pippa why he was on the island when Rafe had asked if he would share his story. Pippa was a lovely person, and she listened sympathetically.

'Would you like a woman's point of view?' she'd asked before she'd left them at the house to go down and meet with Eliza.

'I would.' He nodded. 'Please.'

'From what I saw in the brief time I saw you both together last night, its obvious that Tess is not immune to you.'

'That's one way to put it,' Zac said sadly. 'She hates me for what happened. And I don't blame her.'

'My advice? You've found her, and she knows you want to talk to her.'

'That's right.'

'I'd give her some space. We don't need you here for about two weeks. Go back to Hamo, and as hard as it might be, chill. She knows you're around, and she'll eventually be curious to hear what you've got to say. I admire her; she's obviously a strong person. We had no idea she'd been through that trauma. She never mentioned a word.'

'Perhaps I shouldn't have told you,' Zac said. 'I'm hopeless at handling stuff like this.'

'Don't worry,' Pippa said. 'Rafe and I won't tell a soul. And if you would prefer that Tess doesn't know that we know, I'll forget you've told me anything this morning.'

'Thank you. You've given me some hope.'

Pippa reached for Rafe's hand as Zac watched. 'Do you love her?' she asked.

He nodded. 'I do. Not being able to find her almost did my head in.'

'So if that's how you feel, you never give up. Give it two weeks and come looking for her again, and I guarantee she'll listen. Now I have to get down to the pool and see what's happening.'

Rafe jumped up. 'Are you okay to walk down there.'

Zac saw the warning look that Pippa threw at Rafe. 'Of course, I am. It's not that hot. I won't be long.'

Rafe had stared after her as she'd left and Zac noted that he didn't relax until she was down the hill and out of sight.

'Thanks for the ear, mate,' he said to Rafe as they stood at the top of the steps. 'I'll do what Pippa suggests. If you need me, you know where my boat's moored.'

'And you still want it kept quiet that you're Zac Montgomery and that *Myr* is yours?'

Zac nodded. 'Yes, please. Until I get Tess to listen to me, anyway.'

'Rightio,' Rafe said. He held his hand out and shook Zac's hand. 'Good luck. Keep me in the loop and let us know when you're coming back over.'

'I will. And can I ask you one thing?'

'Of course.'

'If it looks like Tess is going to do a runner, let me know. Now that I've found her, I don't want to have to start at the beginning again.'

'Not a problem. We've got a good vantage point of who comes and goes from up here.'

'Thanks, Rafe. I appreciate it.'

'Mate, I went through the same with Pippa when she first moved here. I knew she was the one for me, but it took a night up a tree to convince her. When you and Tess get sorted, I'll tell you the story.'

'I'll hold you to that. I'll go back to my boat now.'

'That reminds me,' Rafe said as they walked to the gate together. 'Why *Myr*? She's new, isn't she, and you named her?'

Zac nodded. '*Myr*? My Reeza. That's what Tess's name was before she disappeared.'

Chapter 25
Tess – four weeks later.

Christmas had been and gone on Pentecost Island and January had flown by. The Riccardo team had worked and had only taken Christmas Day and Boxing Day off. The pool had been finished and was waiting for the concrete to cure before it was filled. The bar building was taking shape and the day beds had been constructed on the edge of the pool.

Tess was at a loss. Work had been frantic, but she still had time at night to worry and to wonder. The resort had been at full capacity over the Christmas period and the bookings were coming in constantly. Nell and Nat's wedding was only two weeks away, and preparations were in full swing.

Nell was ging to take a week off and fly to Brisbane with Tamsin and Pippa to buy their wedding clothes, and Pippa had put Tess in charge of the office.

Her confidence had had a huge boost from that, and the week had been so busy learning more about the office, she'd crashed into bed at night and not had time to think about Zac, although she had dreamed about him every night.

Since she had decided to listen to him, he'd disappeared. There's been no sign of him on the island, and she'd worried that he'd left.

It was strange. For the past two years Zac Montgomery had been the bad person in her thoughts, and she had let that consume her. But the Zac who had tried to speak to her a month ago was the same Zac she had fallen in love with two years ago and not the monster in her dreams.

A couple of days before the girls headed to Brisbane, Pippa came down to the office to take Tess through some things she wanted done. Tess had forced a casual note into her voice as she took the opportunity that presented itself.

'The pay run is automatic,' Pippa had said. 'Just get Angus to confirm the hours of the kitchen hands, and enter them where Nell showed you, and then everything from the pay slip emails to the bank deposit is automated. Eliza will check the house maid hours and confirm them with you.'

Tess swallowed. 'What about the lifeguard. Are his hours the same?'

'Monty? We decided to put off

his starting date until the pool is filled. He was happy to wait until then.' Pippa lifted her head from the printout she was checking and smiled. 'If he comes over before we get back, just get him to let you know the hours he works. I'll make you his supervisor and Dylan's. Good experience for you. You can keep it on after we come back from Brisbane, because Nell will take a couple of weeks off around the wedding, and then she'll be off having the bub.' She looked at Tess curiously. 'Are you happy with that? Can you handle it?'

Tess swallowed and nodded, even though her heart sank. 'Ah yes, like you say. Good experience,' she said briskly. 'Yes, I can handle that.'

'Excellent. The staff quarters

are just waiting for the carpet to be laid the day before we get back, and then you can all move up there. And that means Isla, the new beauty therapist will start work, and we'll convert the bedrooms off the eastern veranda into Odessa's boutique. It might get a bit noisy in here when Danny and Renzo are knocking walls out. And when the store is done, they're going to make a start on Tam and Gabe's, and Nell and Nate's houses.'

'Wow,' Tess said. 'Never a dull moment here.'

'So you'll be right while we're gone?' Pippa put the files in the desk drawer.

'I will. I'm looking forward to the extra responsibility.'

'Excellent.' Pippa stood and crossed to the door. 'Now there's only one more thing.'

Tess looked up from the keyboard. 'Yes?'

'I want you to take tomorrow off, and go over to Hamo. You're going to be working hard, and it'll be a day for *you.*'

'Oh. I don't need that,' Tess protested.

Pippa's smile was crafty. 'I have an ulterior motive. I'd like some more brochures dropped over there, and I know Jiminy's busy. I've printed them out. If you go over with him in the morning, and drop them off to the places on the list I've put with them, that would be a great help. And then shout yourself a rest day. Get your hair cut or shop, whatever you need to do. You deserve it, Tess. You've worked hard for us over the past three months, and I want you to know it's appreciated.'

Heat filled Tess's cheeks and she blinked away the moisture that filled her eyes.

'Thank you. That's a lovely thing to say.' She pulled a face. 'I've never been thanked in the workplace before. You know you'll never get rid of me now.'

'I'm pleased to hear that. Okay, I'll see you before we leave on Friday. Have a good day tomorrow.'

'Thank you, I will.'

***

Zac

'Thank you. I owe you one, mate.' Zac disconnected the call and stared out from the top deck of his boat. The four weeks that had passed since he'd been on Pentecost Island had dragged, but Rafe's constant reassurance that

Tess was still there had helped him to stay patient. Next week, he would go over and start work there, and he'd been looking forward to it. Rafe's call had filled him with excitement, and he knew that tomorrow would be the day that he would mend bridges and start again with Tess—or it could be the day that he gave up forever. It all depended on if she listened to him, and if she trusted him.

With a deep sigh, he walked down to the galley to throw a meal together. He'd given the crew ten days off, in preparation for the coming weeks when he'd be working on Pentecost Island.

At least he hoped he would. Everything hinged on speaking to Tess tomorrow, and the reception she gave him. He stood at the galley window as his thoughts took

him back to that day two years
ago.

Chapter 26
Zac – two years ago

Zac sat shellshocked as Ken, the security guard, escorted Reeza out to the corridor. Gregor Drummond stood and crossed to the bar in the alcove at the side of the CEO's office.

'An excellent outcome,' Drummond said. 'I thought it might take a lot longer to get to the bottom of that transaction, but the evidence was all there. She did it. I have no doubt.'

Zac leaned forward and stared at the floor as Drummond put a crystal tumbler of whisky in front of him. Something was niggling at him, and he couldn't put his finger in it. The evidence was all there, but his heart and mind were telling him it couldn't be true.

Not his Reeza. No way.

When Drummond had first laid out the evidence for him that proved that Reeza had fraudulently changed the transaction and deposited seven hundred thousand dollars into her account, he had been speechless. Disbelief had rocked him and he'd refused to believe it until the CEO had gone step-by-step through the transaction. He had even produced a time-stamped photo of Reeza at her desk at five-thirty on the afternoon in question.

Zac frowned as he reached for the glass of scotch and took a hefty swig. Why would they have done that? It was the first he'd ever heard of time-stamped photos of workers at their desk. It was just a little bit too convenient. He leaned back in the high-backed chair as Drummond sat opposite him.

'So, that's all behind us now. I'm playing golf this weekend, what are your plans, Montgomery? Would you like to join us?'

My plans? I was going to ask Reeza to move in with me, Zac thought. Before he could say he was busy on the weekend—the last thing he wanted to do was spend it in the CEO's company—the door hidden in the alcove behind him opened and someone walked into the back of the office. Zac was hidden from view but the frown on Drummond's face caught his attention.

The CEO put his hand up as a glass clinked in the bar.

'So the bitch took the fall?' a voice said. 'The journos and cameras are swarming downstairs.'

Zac jumped to his feet and

stared at Bradley Drummond, the CEO's son. 'What did you say?' Zac strode across the room to him.

'Bradley, keep your mouth shut. Don't say another word.' The CEO jumped from his chair, but his son sneered at Zac.

'I said, did the bitch take the fall?'

'That's a strange way to phrase it.' He turned to Drummond. 'How appropriate is it for your son, a minor trader, to know what's going on?'

'How appropriate is it for you to be screwing a minor trader?' Bradley shouted back at him.

As Zac stared at them both, he realised what he'd been trying to remember. 'You're lying. You've framed her, haven't you?' He pointed at Drummond. 'Pick up that phone and tell the police the charges have been dropped. Put it on speakerphone so I can hear you. Now, you bastard!'

Drummond's hand shook as he did as Zac directed.

Once Zac was sure the detective in the foyer had been told the charges against Reeza had been dropped, he raced for the door.

'I'll be back to deal with this in a while. I strongly suggest you don't leave the building.'

He slammed the door behind him and stabbed his finger at the elevator button, hoping and praying that Reeza was still in the foyer with Ken.

Chapter 27

Reeza

The wind blew through Reeza's hair as she stood at the front of Jiminy's launch. She'd taken notice of Pippa's suggestion and had made a hair appointment this afternoon. Not for a cut, but for a colour. It was time to lose the blonde and go back to her natural brunette and grow her hair back. Now that Zac had found her, there was no point in trying to hide behind a different look.

As well as having a haircut, she had decided to seek Zac out while she was on Hamo and listen to what he had to say to her. She'd spent a lot of time thinking about it over the past four weeks, and knew if she had it out with him, she could move on once and for all. At the end of the year when she was due holidays, she'd go back home and visit her parents and the boys.

She'd casually asked Pippa as she'd left yesterday if she knew where Monty lived on Hamilton Island.

'Rafe said he lives near the marina.' Pippa's smile was strange. 'Do you know where the new menu file is?'

It wasn't long before they approached the marina at Hamilton. Tess walked to the wheelhouse, as they turned into the channel. 'Jiminy, do you know a guy called Monty who lives near the marina?' she asked.

'Um.' Another strange look. 'Monty?'

'That's his nickname. His real name is Zac Montgomery.'

'Yeah. Yes, I do. Why do you ask?'

'I want to catch up with him today. He's an old . . . acquaintance.'

Jiminy pointed to the other

side of the marina. 'Yeah, he lives on his boat over there.'

'On his boat? That's not very big.' Tess frowned.

'I wouldn't say no to living on it,' Jiminy said as he brought the launch alongside the wharf. 'Just walk to the end and turn left and you can't miss it.'

'Okay. Thanks. I'll see you at four? Is that when you go over?'

'Yep, four o'clock. You take care today.'

Tess frowned. That was a strange thing to say. 'I will. See you later.' She hoisted her bag over her shoulder and was first off the launch. She'd go down to where Jiminy pointed and try to see Zac first and then the day would be hers.

Her attention was caught by a child squealing as a man pointed to a large batfish that had come right to the edge of the wharf. She watched them feed it bread for a while, and looked up as she walked along the concourse.

Her breath caught as she saw the tall man in denim shorts and a black T-shirt waiting where the wharf joined the path. Composing herself, Tess ignored the thudding of her heart and walked casually over to him. 'Hello, Zac. I was coming to look for you. Jiminy said you live on your boat down there.' She waved in the direction that Jiminy had told her.

'Yes. Yes. I do.' He nodded tersely. 'Let's go and have a coffee somewhere.' His words were clipped and he seemed ill at ease.

Tess's heart sank. Maybe he didn't want to talk to her anymore. Just when she had herself all geared up for it. 'It's okay. If you had something else to do, it's fine. I have all day. Or it doesn't matter. We don't have to talk if you don't want to anymore.'

He took her arm and his fingers were warm against her skin. 'Tess, I have been standing here waiting for you to arrive for almost an hour. I'm not letting you out of my sight until you hear what I have to say.'

She stared up at him. 'How did you know I was coming?'

'Rafe called me.'

'Why would he do that?'

'I'll be honest with you. And I want you to know that every word I tell you today is the honest truth. Rafe and Pippa know our story.'

'Our story?' Her voice came out in a squeak. 'What story?'

'What you need to hear.'

'Do I want to hear this "story"?'

'I sincerely hope so.' He let go of her arm and ran his hand through his hair. 'Okay, honesty all around. We'll start with honesty straight up. We'll have coffee on the boat and then you can scream and yell at me if you want to.'

'Okay. But only a quick coffee. I have things to do here.' Tess was cautious. They would be too close in the confines of that small boat.

'Okay. *Myr* is down here.'

'*Myr*?' she said looking up at him. If she didn't know better, he looked even bigger and more muscled than he had a month ago.

Zac's gaze was intense as it pinned hers. 'When I got my dream boat, I called her *Myr. My Reeza.'*

Her heart set up a slow and steady beat as she looked at him. 'Why would you do that?'

'Because of the way I felt about you. That Friday night when everything went to shit, I was going to ask you to move in with me.'

Tess widened her eyes. '"Went to shit?" I suppose that's one way of saying you accused me of fraud.'

Zac lifted both his hands. 'Wait. Let's just wait until we can sit down and I'll start at the beginning.'

Tess nodded and didn't speak as she followed him along the concourse. They might as well have been kilometres apart. The tension was palpable as she kept her distance. She clutched her bag to her chest as she followed him.

At the last wharf Zac turned to the left and Tess stared at the only boat that was rocking in the gentle swell.

'Bloody hell,' she whispered as she read *Myr* on the side of the luxury cruiser. 'You got your dream. I thought we were going to the boat you had at Rafe's wharf.'

'I got half my dream,' he said quietly. 'But not the most important part.'

The water lapping against the hull of the huge white luxury cruiser was a deep aquamarine, even in the small finger wharves of the Hamilton Island Marina. Dwarfing all of the other boats along the boardwalks, the white boat sat there enticing tourists who milled around, looking up and admiring the vessel. Finally the dark weight that had filled Tess over the past two years began to lift, and she, too, looked up at the massive power cruiser and anticipation filled her with hope.

Zac wouldn't have brought her here unless he had something good to tell her. If he still believed she was guilty he wouldn't have chased her to the Whitsunday Islands.

He led her to the back of the boat and they stepped onto the timber swimming platform. 'Welcome,' he said.

Her voice shook as she answered. 'It's good to be here . . . I think.'

'Have faith in me, Reeza, please.'

Tears stung at her eyes when he called her Reeza. She cleared her throat and nodded. Words failed her. Fear and anticipation mixed together as she followed Zac up a set of polished timber steps. Her eyes widened as she took in the luxury boat. 'You did it, you really did it,' she whispered. 'You left the bank?'

'After what they did to you, I couldn't stay.' Again he raised his hand. 'Wait until we sit down. Let me start at the beginning.'

Tess was torn. After two years of blaming Zac and hating him in her mind—but never in her heart and dreams—she was wondering what had really happened. She was beginning to doubt her perception of the events of that day.

No words were spoken as they stepped onto the top deck. Tess shook her head. A timber bar divided the main living area from a formal dining area. A table setting for two was laid out on the huge glass topped table. Elegant glasses caught the morning sunlight that streamed in through the large windows. Plush white leather sofas formed a square around a circular glass table at the end of the spacious room with some colourful throw rugs over the soft sofas.

Finally Tess breathed the words. 'Oh my God, this is stunning.'

Zac took her hand and led her to the white leather sofa. 'Sit down. Do you want a coffee?"

Tess shook her head. 'No, thank you. I want you to talk to me. Tell me what you need to say.'

With a sigh, Zac sat opposite her on the second double sofa. 'I want you to listen and no comments, reactions or questions until I finish. Okay?'

Tess nodded, overwhelmed by her surroundings. 'Okay.'

She listened as Zac took her through the events of that

afternoon. The audit trail of her login, the time-stamped photograph, the supposed proof that she had transferred the money to her account.

'I knew it was wrong,' he said quietly, 'but it wasn't until bloody Bradley Drummond came in gloating that I realised what I was trying to remember.'

'What was that?' she asked, her eyes glued to his.

'It was the fifteenth of the month. The night that I picked you up at Brentwood, when you got off the train and were caught in the rain. They alleged they had a time stamped video of you at your desk at five thirty-seven. It was fraudulent because I knew you were on the train at that time, because I picked you up at Brentwood.'

Tess nodded. 'That was the night that Bradley Drummond offered to complete a Swiss transaction for me. My big mistake.'

'I knew it wasn't you as soon as they accused you. Drummond didn't show me the evidence until you were about to be called in. I didn't get a chance to think and the date didn't register.'

Tess shook her head from side to side as she stared at him. 'Why?'

'Let me finish. If you hate me for this, so be it, but I want you to know every thought I had when he showed me that "evidence". I doubted you for a minute, Reeza. I thought you had made sure I bumped into you that night to somehow use me, and then I thought of you, the woman I had fallen in love with, and how sweet and innocent and honest you were, and how I knew you wouldn't have done that. But I did doubt you for a moment.'

'There was evidence, Zac,' Tess said quietly as emotion tumbled through her.

'They set you up. It was Bradley Drummond, his father knew that. He came in gloating and didn't see me there. I challenged them and they crumbled. I made him call the foyer and tell Ken to tell the police to drop the charges and then I ran out looking for you, but when I got summoned to the police station I tried to call you but your phone didn't connect?'

Tess fought the happiness and relief that was stealing over her. 'You believed in me?'

'Of course I did. But I couldn't find you. Where did you go?'

'I was on a train to Brisbane the next morning. Mum met me at Central. I was so upset because I thought you believed them.'

'When you didn't answer your phone I called your home and they wouldn't tell me.'

'I was so scared of the media tracking me. I took the SIM card out of my mobile and put it in the rubbish bin on the train. I bought a new one when I got to Brisbane.'

Zac hesitated; he sat back on the sofa and looked at her and his expression almost broke her heart. 'I've searched for you for almost two years. I wasn't going to give up.'

'You believed in me. You believed in me all that time.' Tess swallowed, and then she stood and crossed to where Zac sat. 'That's going to take some getting used to.'

He stood and opened his arms. 'Sweetheart. I vowed not to stop until I found you.'

She stepped towards him and as Zac's arms held her close, the past two years faded to nothing. Reeza had come home to the place she wanted to be.

Epilogue
Pippa - February 14

A crowd had gathered around our new pool on Pentecost Island on Valentine's Day. The water glinted in the morning sunlight, and the weather gods had put on a spectacular day for us. The expanse of water out to the horizon was the usual sapphire blue. As always lately, the huts were booked to capacity and the guests stood on the other side of the pool. Rafe and I had decided to have it filled last night so that it was a surprise for everyone when they arrived for our official "first splash" at nine a.m. That way everyone could be there before they started work for the day.

Evie and Jed were on the island. Evie had come back to help Dylan with the final landscaping, and they had done a superb job. Full grown tropical shrubs in bloom edged the paths, and surrounded the bar.

I smiled as my gaze swept over the group waiting for our new lifeguard to do the honours. At the girls' sunset drinks on the beach last Friday night, I had asked for a vote on who should do the first dive into the pool at our opening.

Tess had blushed as the winning vote was cast for Zac, with Rafe and Philippe tying for a close second.

I had been so happy the day before I flew to Brisbane two weeks earlier with Nell and Tamsin when Zac had brought Tess back over to the island.

Rafe and I had been on our balcony and he'd smiled when he drew my attention to the couple who had come in by tender to our wharf.

I looked down as Zac took Tess into his arms and kissed her thoroughly, and then my gaze had lifted to the white cruiser moored outside the bay.

A soft sigh had escaped my lips. 'Another happy couple on our island.'

Zac and Tess had been inseparable ever since, and Zac's boat was now a permanent feature outside our bay. To our surprise once he'd sorted things with Tess, Zac had asked if he could stay on and do the lifeguard and bar job.

Now he and Rafe stood in the middle of the narrow walkway between the pool and the waters of the Whitsunday Passage. Tess and Cherry held the bright pink ribbon that went along the length of the path. Rafe was doing the official opening and cutting the ribbon, and then Zac—looking very tanned and muscular—was diving into the pool.

Happiness filled me as I looked around at the staff.

My *friends.*

Tam and Gabe, Nell and Nat, Eliza, Evie and Jed, Angus, Odessa and Dylan, Sienna and Danny stood together. Renzo Riccardo and his wife had come across for the opening too.

Our island was almost complete.

I had recovered physically and emotionally from my recent miscarriage, and was looking forward to being pregnant again soon. I had faith that it would happen and I had managed to shed my doubts with Rafe's love and support.

We were all looking forward to Nell and Nat's wedding in two weeks, and I know Sienna was excited about the arrival of Isla who was due on Jiminy's launch this morning.

Rafe held the microphone up and I shivered as my husband's deep voice with the gorgeous accent filled the air. I smiled; he was good with the written word, but Rafe hated speaking in public, so his speech was short and sweet.

'It gives me great pleasure to declare Ma Carmichael's pool open. Zac, over to you.'

I glanced at Tess as Zac stepped up onto the short springboard. The love on her face was clear to see, and it brought a smile to my lips.

Zac walked to the end of the board and stood on his toes. He looked up and lifted a hand to his lips and blew a kiss to Tess. My smile widened as a collective sigh came from the girls. He was a fine looking man.

As Zac executed a perfect dive into the pool, a cheer went up and champagne corks popped. Rafe had insisted that it wasn't too early to celebrate the pool opening with mimosas. Dylan and Angus were soon walking around with trays.

A hooter sounded and I looked across to the east of the bay. Jiminy's launch was early.

I frowned as a tall girl with dark hair climbed onto the top of Jiminy's wheelhouse and waved madly.

'Sienna,' I called. 'Isla's arrived.'

THE END

I hope you are enjoying the stories of Pentecost Island where romance entices and secrets unfold. The series wraps up with Isla's story.

Irish dreams or island dreams?
Isla's secret is the biggest one of all. Will Pentecost Island be the place where she comes to terms with her past?
Ronan Doyle has searched for Isla for a long time. Will he be the key to her happiness or will her secret past ruin their chance of a happy ever after?

You can find Isla's story here in eBook
books2read.com/u/3yzYYL

or in print here
https://www.annieseaton.net/store.html

Other Books
Whitsunday Dawn
Undara
Osprey Reef (2021)

Porter Sisters Series

Kakadu Sunset

Daintree

Diamond Sky

Hidden Valley

Pentecost Island Series
(2020)

Pippa

Eliza

Nell

Tamsin

Evie

Cherry

Odessa

Sienna

Tess

Isla

Sunshine Coast Series

Waiting for Ana

The Trouble with Jack

Healing His Heart

Bondi Beach Love Series

Beach House

Beach Music

Beach Walk

Beach Dreams

The House on the Hill

Second Chance Bay Series

Her Outback Playboy

Her Outback Protector

Her Outback Haven

Her Outback Paradise

Love Across Time Series

Come Back to Me

Follow Me

Finding Home

The Threads that Bind

Others

The Trouble with Paradise

Deadly Secrets

Adventures in Time

Silver Valley Witch

The Emerald Necklace

Worth the Wait

Ten Days in Paradise

About the Author

Finalist for the NZ KORU award 2018 and 2020.

Winner ... Best Established Author of the Year 2017 AUSROM

Long listed for the Sisters in Crime Davitt Awards 2016, 2017, 2018, 2019

Finalist in Book of the Year, Long Romance, RWA Ruby awards 2016

Winner ... Best Established Author of the Year 2015 AUSROM
Winner ... Author of the Year 2014 AUSROM

Best Established Author, Ausrom Readers' Choice 2017

Book of the Year (Whitsunday Dawn) Ausrom Readers' Choice Awards 2018

Annie lives in Australia, on the beautiful north coast of New South

Wales. She sits in her writing chair and looks out over the tranquil Pacific Ocean. She has fulfilled her lifelong dream of becoming an author and is producing books at a prolific rate.

She writes contemporary romance and loves telling the stories that always have a happily ever after. She lives with her very own hero of many years and they share their home with Toby, the naughtiest dog in the universe, and Barney, the rag doll kitten, who hides when the grandchildren come to visit.

Stay up to date with her latest releases at her website: http://www.annieseaton.net